THE
Night Walkers

Also by Otto Coontz
MYSTERY MADNESS

THE
Night Walkers

Otto Coontz

Houghton Mifflin Company
Boston 1982

Library of Congress Cataloging in Publication Data
Coontz, Otto.
    The night walkers.

    Summary: When half of the children of Covendale are
struck down by a mysterious illness, only two thirteen-
year-old girls and a housekeeper suspect the infection
is destroying the children's souls as well as their
bodies.
    [1. Horror — Fiction]   I. Title.
PZ7.C7845Ni   [Fic]   82-6161
ISBN 0-395-32557-9   AACR2

*For Stephen McCauley, Diane Leary,
and for my brother Eric*

Contents

Fall, leaves, fall; die, flowers, away;
    Lengthen night and shorten day;
Every leaf speaks bliss to me
Fluttering from the autumn tree.
I shall smile when wreaths of snow
Blossom where the rose should grow;
I shall sing when night's decay
Ushers in a drearier day.

        "Fall, Leaves, Fall," by
        Emily Brontë

THE
Night Walkers

1

The Day the Birds Fell from the Sky

NORA PULLED UP her collar against the chilly October wind and tucked her chin in turtlelike, burrowing her hands in her pockets. She felt cold and conspicuous sitting alone on the bench in front of school, but she'd promised Maxine she'd wait. A few feet away, Audrey Quinn and several of her friends chatted noisily as they watched the eighth grade boys play football. Nora glanced at them furtively, slumping lower in the bench. She adjusted her glasses and tried to follow the game.

Across the school yard, a solitary gull glided above the trees. Shivering and pulling her jacket tighter, Nora gazed after the bird when suddenly the gull faltered, dropping lower in the gray sky. It bobbed and zigzagged through the treetops, then plummeted from sight. Must be hurt, Nora thought, still watching for the bird. After a moment, she shrugged and turned back to the game.

Peter Wade plowed across the muddy school yard with Nora's brother Tony on his heels. Just as Peter reached the goal, Tony lunged, nicking the boy's back and falling to his knees.

"I tagged you, Wade!" Tony shouted as he jumped back up with grass and dirt smeared across his jeans.

"I was over!" Peter shouted back breathlessly.

"Not before I tagged you!"

"Did not, Lane! *I* didn't feel it!"

"That's what you always say!"

"He tagged you, Pete. Don't be a sore loser," Audrey called out, taking advantage of the situation to score a few points with Tony. Suddenly, slamming a stack of books down on the bench, Maxine appeared and collapsed beside Nora.

"What took you so long?" Over Maxine's shoulder, Nora could see Miss Schumann heavily descend the stairs, her briefcase stuffed with manila folders and her great black pocketbook jerking against her hip.

"Schumann said I couldn't make it up." Maxine sighed. "What a witch."

Nora nudged her, darting her eyes to the side. "She's right behind you." Maxine stiffened, shifting her long legs and glancing over her shoulder. They waited in silence till their teacher turned the corner of the building.

"You just can't win," Maxine griped. "If I'd finished the composition, I couldn't have studied for the math quiz. So I studied for the quiz, and what happens? I flunk it anyway, and then Schumann gives me an incomplete in English Comp."

Nora looked distracted. Maxine could tell she was no longer listening. Audrey's voice carried across the yard. She was talking about a party. A Halloween costume party.

"Any of you want to help with the invitations?" Audrey was asking her friends. "I'd like to mail them out tomorrow."

Nora would have been eager to volunteer, but she knew the remark hadn't been meant for her.

"Do you think she'll invite us?" she whispered to Maxine.

"Who knows? You can never tell who's on Quinn's hate list from one day to the next. But you can be sure she'll ask you if she's going to ask Tony. And we *know* how she feels about Tony." Maxine clasped her hands to her chest and slumped back on the bench in a swoon. Nora smiled to herself. Sometimes, having Tony for a brother had its points. Maxine sat up and glanced across the field.

"Hey, are you watching this game?"

Nora shrugged.

"I didn't think so. Come on, it's too cold to sit around here." Maxine and Nora gathered up their books and started across the school yard. Nora quickened her pace to keep up with her long-legged friend. The shouts from the boys playing football faded as they turned down Center Street.

"Max," Nora said thoughtfully, "what if she *doesn't* invite me? Ever since school started, she's acted like I don't even exist."

"Don't sweat it. It's obvious she still has a crush on Tony."

"What about you? What if she asks me and doesn't ask you?"

"Maybe you could go as a football." Maxine grinned. "Then I could borrow Tony's uniform and sneak in as your date."

"Oh, great!" Nora sighed. "Just what I always wanted to be. A football!"

The two girls parted at the corner of Center and Main. Nora's pace slowed as she approached Bergdorff's Bakery. She jingled the change in her pocket and stood indecisively before the window with its enticing display of pastries. One cream cheese brownie, she thought, how much difference could one little brownie make? Catching her reflection in the glass, Nora sighed and reluctantly moved on. It makes a difference, she assured herself, a difference of four hundred calories. If she didn't watch herself, she thought wryly, she *would* show up at Audrey's party looking like a football. Assuming she'd be invited, she reminded herself, crossing her fingers in her pocket. Picking up her pace again, she began to think of costume ideas.

As she turned down Willoughby Street, something in the gutter caught her eye. When she got closer, she saw that it was a gull. Another one, she thought with dismay. What's going on with the gulls? Curiously, she watched the bird flutter on its side in a feeble attempt to get off the ground. Nora stepped back as the bird flopped over, then suddenly caught her breath. The area beneath the wing on one side was gouged open. Over the wound, odd little blisters were forming. Out of the corner of her eye, Nora caught a glimpse of the Cravens' cat skulking along the hedges.

"Darn Nikki," she muttered angrily, watching the cat prowl into the shadows of the neighbor's garage. Suddenly the cat shook convulsively and began to cough something up. Serves him right, Nora thought, glancing again at the gull. The bird grew still. Nora turned and crossed the street.

*

"Mom?" Nora called out as she closed the door behind her.

"Up here!" Mrs. Lane answered from her study. Nora lumbered up the stairs and down to the room at the end of the hall. Her mother sat with her back to the door, typing up an article for the Covendale weekly. Sensing Nora's presence, she stopped typing and turned in her chair.

"What's up?"

"Mom, I just saw a dead gull in the street out front of Cravens' yard."

"That's odd." Mrs. Lane looked thoughtful.

"What do you mean?" Nora leaned in the doorway.

"When I was driving out to the dump this morning, a gull flew into the windshield."

"Well, this one didn't fly into any windshield. The

5

Cravens' cat got to it. I can't stand that cat. Why is he always killing things?" Nora unzipped her jacket and took it off. Her brow wrinkled moodily.

"It's instinct, dear. Don't let it upset you. All cats do it." Janet Lane swiveled her chair around and stuck a clean sheet into the typewriter. "I'd better get back to work. I still have to proof this thing before I start supper."

Nora went back downstairs to her room and began to make a list of costume ideas. Before long, she heard the front door close. She pushed her chair back and started off toward the kitchen.

Tony's books were stacked on the kitchen table. His legs stuck out from beneath the refrigerator door. Nora walked up behind him.

"Did Aud say anything to you about Halloween?"

"Huh?" Tony turned to face her, a chunk of banana bread in one hand and a quart of milk in the other. It always irked Nora when he drank right out of the carton.

"I saw her talking to you at football practice. Didn't she say anything about Halloween?" Nora watched the banana bread vanish in three bites. Why could Tony eat like a horse and never gain an ounce? For twins, she mused, the only thing they had in common was their birthday.

"Quinn? She wasn't talking to me. She caught Pete Wade trying to steal a goal. Did you see it? I tagged him four feet from the goal and he denied it. If he missed a pass he'd try to blame it on the wind. If he missed the goal he'd try to convince you somebody moved it. That guy would try anything. A real sport!" Tony flopped into a chair and opened his book on the table. It was a book on hockey. Food and sports, Nora thought with disdain, were the only things Tony cared about. Crumbs of banana bread fell over the pages of Tony's book. Nora shrugged and trudged back to her room.

*

An hour later, Tony was still sitting there, engrossed in his hockey book while Nora tried to set the table.

"Come on, Tony, would you move the books? It's the kitchen, not the public library."

Tony gathered up his books and moved them to the counter.

"Please, not here, Tony," Mrs. Lane warned. "I'm trying to make dinner." As she turned the hamburgers in the skillet, the phone rang. She grabbed the receiver from the wall. "Hello?" she answered, then turned to the twins. "It's Marty Craven. He wants to know if either of you has seen Nikki."

"Not since this afternoon, when I saw that dead gull," Nora answered. "Tell him to check his garage." Her mother relayed this to Marty then hung up.

"Mom." Tony leaned against the counter while his mother piled the meat on a platter. "I was just thinking. Maybe we should have a cat."

"Oh?" Mrs. Lane wrinkled her nose, sniffing and picking up pot lids. "I did it again," she muttered, grabbing a pan of scorched rice.

"I think it'd be nice to have a pet," Tony continued, "and it'd keep you company while you worked."

"I don't need any more company while I work." Mrs. Lane scraped the burned rice into the sink. "I have you two." She smiled.

"Well, *I'd* still like to have one. Please, Mom?"

"First, I'd like to know who would take care of this cat. Who'd feed it and clean up after it?" The water from the faucet hissed as it filled the scorched pan.

"Well, I thought since you're here all the time . . ."

"That's just what I thought you thought." Mrs. Lane raised one eyebrow. "Tony, I have enough to do cleaning up after you two. Come, my pets, chow time."

"But Mom," Tony persisted, "a cat's not any trouble. You'd hardly know it was here. Nikki spends most of the time outdoors, and when he's inside, he just uses a kitty litter box."

Nora pinched her nose dramatically. "That's all we need. Another gull killer in the neighborhood."

"Someone still has to feed it and clean its box." Mrs. Lane passed Tony his plate.

"And where would we keep its litter box?" Nora added. "I've been to the Cravens'. *They* keep it in the kitchen. Right where everyone eats. And it always smells, the whole house, the minute you open the door. Pretty gross, if you ask me. And I can already tell you what Dad'll say. 'You know how many viruses cats carry?' "

"Butt out, Nora. No one asked you. And you don't know what Dad's going to say."

"Come on, let's eat while it's hot." Mrs. Lane glanced meaningfully at both of them as she pulled out her chair and sat down.

*

Before going to bed, Nora spent twenty minutes leaning over the bathroom sink and studying her face in the mirror. It resembled her father's, thick featured and dark, framed with curly brown hair. She smeared Clearasil an eighth of an inch thick over a bump on her chin.

"Why me?" she asked the bump. "With twenty billion kids in the world, why did you have to pick on me?"

"Nora, you've been in there half the night," her mother called through the door. "Please hurry it up, I want to soak a sweater in the sink."

Nora stuck her glasses back on and turned to open the door. "Mom, how do you think I'd look with straight hair?"

"The grass is always greener." Mrs. Lane squeezed past Nora with detergent in one hand and the sweater in the other. "Curls suit you, dear."

"Sure, every time it rains it looks like I got electrocuted." Nora sat on the edge of the tub.

Mrs. Lane laughed. "That's a look women are paying fifty dollars a throw for. Consider yourself lucky."

"Some luck." Nora sighed. "I look just like dad."

"I think your father's quite handsome."

"That's what I mean. It's fine for him and Tony, but for a girl? And my chin looks like the state of Washington.

Look here." Nora pointed at the bump. "Mount Saint Helens."

Mrs. Lane turned off the faucet. "Nora, everyone goes through it. It's part of growing. It's just a phase."

"Some phase. I've been starving myself for a month and I've only lost four pounds. You know what Max said today? I ought to dress up as a football for Halloween. A *football!*" Nora frowned.

"Rome wasn't built in a day." Her mother smiled. "It took thirteen years to get the way you are now. Be patient; no one changes overnight. Remember the tale of the ugly duckling? There's a swan in there." Mrs. Lane tapped the space over Nora's heart.

"You mean an ostrich," Nora grumbled. Her mother smiled warmly.

"My mother called it the cocoon stage. Believe me, it'll be worth the wait."

"How long a wait?" Nora glanced at her wrist watch, trying to keep a straight face.

"I don't know." Her mother squeezed detergent into the sink. "But while you're waiting, you want to wash out this sweater?"

Nora laughed and ducked out the door.

*

After dumping her clothes in the hamper, Nora walked out to the living room to say good night to her father. Dr. Lane was sprawled across the couch next to Tony, who hunched gloomily in the corner. Looking at him, Nora knew she'd guessed right about her father's reaction. She felt a little guilty, even if she did hate cats.

"Night, Dad," Nora said softly.

Dr. Lane blinked across at her. "Night, honey."

After a moment, Nora looked down at the end of the couch where Tony sat huddled.

"I'm sorry. About getting a pet, I mean."

"I bet you are," Tony mumbled without looking up.

"So, what are you two going to do while your mother's at the paper tomorrow?" Dr. Lane stood and stretched.

"Max might come over," Nora answered.

"Tony?"

"Probably just hang out with Marty."

"Well, I know it's not a school day tomorrow, but it's late. Bedtime, kids."

2

Cecil's Garden

HAS NIKKI COME back yet?" Mr. Craven asked the house-keeper Saturday morning.

"I left his bowl out on the backstairs," Mrs. Cribbins answered. "Look and see if he's eaten."

Mr. Craven went out the back door and returned a moment later. "Hasn't touched it. I wonder where he's gone?"

"Don't worry about him." The housekeeper looked up from the table, where she was peeling apples for a pie. "I've swept enough feathers off the back stoop to know that cat can fend for himself. He'll be back when he's good and ready."

"I suppose you're right." Mr. Craven picked the shopping list up from the table and walked out to the hall. He shouted up the stairs, "Marty? I'm leaving now!" After a few moments Marty bounded down followed by Tony.

"Would you boys get the trash from under the sink? I

thought we'd stop at the dump first. Those papers have been piling up."

"Don't you go filling your face with junk food, young man. I'm planning a nice dinner," Mrs. Cribbins warned as Martin dragged the plastic trash bags out from under the sink.

"I won't, don't sweat it." Martin winked at Tony, knowing he could always count on his father to stop for ice cream.

"Watch your tongue," Mrs. Cribbins called after him.

The boys loaded the rubbish into the station wagon and climbed in front. Tony sat by the window.

"Maybe we'll see old Cecil McNab," Martin whispered conspiratorially. "The guy gets loonier every day. Last time we were out there, he told Dad the gulls were dropping right out of the sky."

"What?"

"Marty," Mr. Craven said sternly, "if we run into Cecil, no shenanigans."

"Aw, Dad. He's just an old crank."

"Maybe so. But the man has feelings, just like anybody else. It doesn't hurt to be kind."

"How can you be kind to a guy who sits around taking pot shots at gulls all day? It makes me sick."

"At least they die quickly. Better than those new pesticides he's been spraying around the dump."

"So, why doesn't he just leave them alone?"

"They're scavengers, and it's Cecil's job to look after the place."

"I still don't see why he has to kill them. It's not like they're bothering anyone. They just eat junk that people throw away."

"I know, son. It doesn't make much sense. But Cecil runs the dump and it's really none of our business."

Tony watched the trees rush by as the car turned off Willoughby Street and picked up speed on the wide country road. He rolled his window down slightly and rested his head on the back of the seat. Closing his eyes, he listened to the sounds from the fields. The crisp October air carried the smell of the sea.

With his eyes closed, sniffing the salty air, Tony pictured the shoreline. Although it was only a ten-minute drive, he rarely got to go to the beach. His father had a typical doctor's schedule, and his mother was usually holed up in the second-floor den pecking away at her typewriter. At least, Tony thought, he *had* a mother. All Martin had was his father. Although Mr. Craven's real estate office was in his home, and although he spent a lot of time with Martin, Tony knew it wasn't the same.

A seagull shrieked overhead and the air altered slightly. Tony wrinkled his nose at the pungent scent of seaweed baking in the sun and the unmistakable smell of decomposing fish. As the car neared the dump, the smell became assaulting.

Martin nudged him. "Hey, are you falling asleep?" Tony kept his eyes closed. ·

"I want to see if I can tell where we are without looking."

"You mean like that game 'Blind Guess'?"

"Sort of."

"All right then, where are we?"

"It smells like the dump's right ahead. But it must be a little way off yet, because I still don't hear the gulls."

"Wrong!" Martin announced as the car slowed down. "We're already at the dump." Tony snapped open his eyes and saw hills of rubbish glistening in the sun like mounds of jewels. As the car drove through the gate, the jewels turned into broken glass and bits of aluminum foil and tin. The air was permeated with a sweet musty smell.

"Where are the gulls?" Tony glanced around at the rubble.

Martin pointed. "There's a couple, on top of that heap."

"But this place is usually swarming with them." Tony watched the two birds cackle at one another, bickering over some moldy scrap. As Mr. Craven opened the car door they took to the air.

"Tony's right. It's never been this quiet." Martin's father searched the sky down by the shoreline. "Maybe there's a big school of fish running the shoals."

"They probably just got tired of old Cecil taking pot shots at them," Marty whispered, glancing nervously over his shoulder. "I wonder where the old guy is?"

"I'll go find him and see where he wants us to put the papers." Mr. Craven walked off through the maze of rubbish to search for the attendant. Martin turned to Tony.

"Let's check out Cecil's garden."

"Garden? Here?" Tony couldn't imagine anything growing in the middle of this rubble.

"Cecil started one last summer. He told my dad that food scraps make better fertilizer than you can buy. Come on, I'll show you." The two boys walked along the fence that separated the dump from the marshes. A deep pit filled with rotting food stretched for several yards between the hills of rubbish. The stench was nearly unbearable. Tony cupped his hands over his face and hurried past it.

"It's disgusting. How can he stand to live out here?"

"Somebody has to take care of the place. Over here." Martin walked ahead, past empty drums of pesticides and mounds of plastic waste to the garden. Tony was surprised to see the even rows of carrots this late in the fall. Behind them, a dozen deep blue morning glories crept along the fence, swaying lazily in the offshore breeze.

*

Across the dump, Mr. Craven was rapping on the attendant's trailer. A buzzing sound drifted through the window.

"Cecil, it's Hartford Craven!" He shouted for the second time. Looking down at the shelter attached to one end of the trailer, he spotted Cecil's dilapidated pickup. It was clear he hadn't gone to town. Then he noticed that the door was ajar. A trail of ants streamed over the cinder-block steps and across the doorsill. On impulse, he pushed the door open. The only light came from the sun behind him, casting his shadow into the narrow hallway that led to two

16

tiny rooms at either end. A television set was on in the room to the right, the screen filled with static. All the window blinds were drawn. His hand felt over the wall for a light switch.

"Bulb must be burned out," he mumbled, flicking it a few times and squinting into the shadows. In the darkness of the bedroom to his left, something stirred.

"Cecil?" There was no reply.

*

"Go on, try one," Martin urged Tony.

"Marty, I hate carrots."

"But they're real sweet when they're fresh. Especially the small ones. Come on, try one." Martin yanked up one the size of his thumb. "Here." Reluctantly, Tony accepted it, nibbling just a bit. When Martin stooped to pull up another, Tony tossed the carrot behind him.

"Well, are they as good as I said they were?" Martin chomped the end off his.

"They're O.K.," Tony answered indifferently. While he carefully stepped over the thick leafy rows to look at a patch of pumpkins, Martin devoured several more carrots.

"Hey, what are you boys up to?"

Martin and Tony jumped, afraid for a moment it was Cecil.

"I was just showing Tony Cecil's garden," Martin answered.

"Looks more like sampling than showing." Mr. Craven grinned, nodding toward the stump of carrot dangling from

Martin's hand and the remnants of others scattered around his feet.

"It's only a few. Cecil's not going to miss them." He stooped to pull another one. "Want one, Dad?"

"No, thanks. Come on, boys, we still have a lot to do."

"Hey, what do you suppose this stuff is?" Martin pushed back the thick leaves of a cabbage, exposing the soil by the roots. A thin mossy growth formed a collar around the plant. It shimmered delicately in the shade of the leaves. When Martin ran his fingers through it, the substance disintegrated like powder. He jerked his hand back. "It tingles. Feels sort of like ice needles." He blew the dust from his fingertips. As it scattered into the wind, it changed from green to a dull gray ash.

"Some type of fungus, like lichen, I suppose. Come on, we have a lot of errands to do."

"Did you find Cecil?" Martin stood, finishing off his last carrot.

"No, but his truck's still here. He probably went fishing." Mr. Craven led the way back to the car. After stacking the rubbish by the gate, he climbed in and started the engine.

"Come on!" Martin called back to Tony, who had picked up a stick and was poking at something in a rubbish heap a few yards away.

"What were you looking at?" Martin asked as he slid in after Tony and slammed the door.

"Just a dead gull." Tony shrugged.

*

While Mr. Craven ran one more errand, Tony and Martin finished off a carton of fried clams on the steps of Sweeney's Hardware. As Martin ate, he thought guiltily of Mrs. Cribbins. It irked him how strict she had become. Before his mother died, Mrs. Cribbins had been so much nicer, even fun at times. Now she was always on his back.

"All the clams gone?" Mr. Craven had just come out of the hardware store.

"What do you mean?" Martin grinned. "You ate most of them before you went into Sweeney's."

"Then I guess it's time for sundaes. I'll race you guys over to Friendly's."

*

As luck would have it, Martin began to feel queasy that night, just as dinner was served. With a frown on his face, he squirmed in his seat, pushing the food around on his plate.

"I can't eat. I have a stomachache." Martin got up from his seat.

Mrs. Cribbins dropped her fork in disgust. "I told you not to fill up on junk, didn't I?" Martin was on his way out of the dining room. He glanced back at her angrily, but said nothing. All he could think of was lying down.

"It's all right, son. Go on, you're excused."

"That's just dandy!" Mrs. Cribbins stood in a huff. "Who cares if I spend half the day putting a meal together?" She waved her hand over the table. "Who cares if the boy eats garbage all day then comes home too sick to touch a proper meal? Go ahead, pamper him. Honestly, I don't know why I bother."

"Ingrid," Mr. Craven interrupted, "all he had was a few clams and some ice cream. And it was my idea in the first place."

"Well, you ought to be ashamed of yourself!"

"Why? I had the same thing and I feel fine."

"You're a grown man. Fried clams and ice cream! No wonder the boy has cramps. I don't understand why you encourage his bad habits. Why don't you let me do my job?"

"Your job, Mrs. Cribbins, is to look after the house and cook. I think I know best how to raise my own son." As soon as Hartford Craven said this he regretted it. Mrs. Cribbins left the table without replying and went up after Martin. She found him lying across his bed with his clothes on.

"Come on, off with them and under the covers. If you're sick you're going to take care of yourself." The housekeeper put her hand to Martin's forehead. The boy brushed it away.

"It's only a stomachache, Mrs. Cribbins. I don't have a fever."

"What do you know about fevers? Now get out of those clothes."

"Not until you leave the room," Martin muttered. He was curled on his side and holding his stomach.

"Do you want me to call your father up here?"

"Call him," Martin said defiantly, wincing with pain.

"I'm not a baby, Mrs. Cribbins. I'm thirteen years old. I can undress myself, and I don't need an audience."

"I'm only trying to help."

"Then leave the room. Please."

The housekeeper stared uncertainly at the boy.

"Go on, I'll get into bed if you leave."

Reluctantly, she stepped back into the hall.

"And close the door," Martin called after her.

Mrs. Cribbins warily returned to the dining room and sat down again. After watching her pick disconsolately at her food, Mr. Craven broke the silence.

"Ingrid, the boy's growing up. You fuss over him as though he were still a small child. You make him feel hedged in."

"I do the best I can." The housekeeper spoke with undisguised pain.

"I know you do," the boy's father said gently, "but sometimes it's just too much. Try to relax and let me worry about Martin. After all, he's all I *have* to worry about."

And they both were all *she* had, the old woman thought to herself, but she could say nothing. She had already overstepped her bounds.

*

Later that night, when they all were in bed, a furry black animal darted through the cat flap into the darkened house. It sniffed the air, prowled softly through the hall, then scurried up the stairs. To the right, the housekeeper's whispered prayers drifted out from behind her closed door. The cat hissed and turned toward the boy's room. Creeping soundlessly through the open door, it leaped onto the foot of the bed. The boy seemed undisturbed by the cat's light step across the blanket. The animal's whiskers brushed his cheek as it curled itself up by the pillow. Martin's hand moved to scratch his face. The cat's claws extended. The boy dropped his hand and rolled onto his back. His jaw fell slack as he breathed more deeply. The cat retracted its claws and watched the boy for a few moments, then cautiously climbed to his chest. Gently it stretched, arching its neck, poised over the sleeping boy's face. It began to breathe in rhythm with the boy, pushing its face even closer. When Martin inhaled the cat exhaled. A stream of luminous dust passed between them.

3

The Face in the Shadows

Nora?" Tony knocked at her door. "Mom said to tell you breakfast is ready."

"I'll be right there!" Nora stretched and yawned, climbing groggily out of bed. She slipped into her robe and shuffled down the hall. Tony was buried behind a sports almanac, noisily slurping his oatmeal. Mrs. Lane sat across from him, frowning over the Times crossword. The kitchen was fragrant with freshly brewed coffee and toasting English muffins. Nora took her seat and stared at her cereal without enthusiasm.

"Can I have some more, Mom?" Tony's face popped up behind his book.

"You've already had seconds, dear."

"But I'm starving. I didn't eat any supper, remember?"

Mrs. Lane put the paper down and went to boil more water.

"That's the last time I eat at Groton's," Tony remarked. "Those were the greasiest clams I've ever had."

"There's nothing wrong with Groton's." His mother measured the rolled oats into the pan. "It's your eating habits. What do you expect after fried clams and a hot fudge sundae?"

"Mom, it was food poisoning. My stomach felt like it was turning inside out. It was wicked."

"I'm sure your stomach was just telling you it had enough. Did Martin get sick too?"

"I don't know. I haven't talked to him yet."

"Well, I see the patient's recovered." Dr. Lane slipped into the seat next to Tony.

"It was food poisoning, wasn't it, Dad?"

"It was too much of the wrong combination of foods. I told you, if it was food poisoning, you'd have had a lot more to worry about than a stomachache."

"Like what?"

"Like the runs, for one."

Nora giggled. The picture this term conjured up in her mind always struck her funny.

"Did I ever tell you about the time my army troop was hit with salmonella? Forty guys to one latrine."

Nora giggled again.

"What's salmonella?" Tony asked. "Sounds like some kind of salami."

"It's a bacterium that grows in chicken if the meat isn't kept hot enough. Goes through you like water. And it hits fast. One minute you're picking at a drumstick, the next . . ."

"Mark," Mrs. Lane interrupted, "we're trying to eat breakfast." Dr. Lane winked at Tony and reached for a section of the newspaper lying in the middle of the table. As Mrs. Lane poured his coffee, the phone rang. She set down the pot and answered it.

"Nora, it's Max," she announced, holding out the kitchen extension. Nora took the phone and leaned against the counter. After a brief pause, she said, "I'll be over as soon as I can," and hung up.

"Nora, you're not finished," her mother called after her as she started out the door.

"Mom, I'm *trying* to *diet!*"

"From the look of your cereal bowl, I'd call it a hunger strike." Her mother sighed. "All right, go ahead."

On the way to her room, Nora suddenly thought of a costume for Audrey's party. She would go as Dracula's Bride. But whoever heard of a four-foot overweight vampire with corkscrew curls? Nora tugged at her hair in the mirror and tried to look seductive. Well, maybe eye make-up would help, she mused. As Nora began to dress, her mother poked her head in the door.

"I have to deliver an article to the *Chronicle*. If you hurry, I'll drop you off at Max's."

"I'll be ready in a sec." Nora tied her shoes, grabbed her coat, and darted down the hall.

*

When Mrs. Cribbins got back from church, she went up to wake Martin and his father for breakfast.

"Martin?" she called softly through the open door. The boy's sheets were tangled and drawn up over his head. Mrs. Cribbins crossed the room to the window and pulled up the blind. It had rained earlier, and the sun was just breaking through the clouds. It filtered brightly through the window. A groan came from Martin's bed.

"Time to get up." She drew the sheet back from the boy's face. "Oh my God." The words barely escaped her lips before the boy ripped the sheet out of her hands and drew it back over himself.

"What happened to your eyes?"

"Close the blind," the boy said flatly, ignoring her question.

"Martin" — Mrs. Cribbins reached toward the shape beneath the sheets — "let me see your face." The boy moved to the edge of the bed, away from her.

"I told you to close the blinds." One of his arms projected from under the sheet. Where the sunlight shone on his hand, an angry red rash appeared. When she reached out to touch it, the boy jerked his hand away.

"Do you want me to get your father?" Martin curled beneath the sheet without replying. Mrs. Cribbins walked briskly from the room and down the hall.

"Mr. Craven!" She knocked loudly on the door.

"Ummm?" A sleepy voice answered from the other side. "What is it?"

"There's something wrong with Martin. His eyelids are swollen, and he's breaking out in some sort of rash." After a moment the door opened and the man stepped out, tying the belt to his robe.

"A rash?" He was rubbing the sleep from his eyes.

"He won't let me touch him." The housekeeper followed Mr. Craven down the hall. "Should I call Dr. Lane?"

"Let me look at him first. I don't want to bother Mark on Sunday unless it's really necessary."

"I don't need a doctor!" Martin shouted when he heard their voices.

"It's all right, Marty. I'm just going to take a look at you." Then, to the housekeeper, he added softly, "Let me go in alone. He sounds a little cranky." The room was in semidarkness. The blinds had been redrawn. Mr. Craven shut the door behind him.

"Don't turn on the light," the boy called hoarsely from his bed.

"Why not? I can hardly see you."

"It hurts my eyes."

"All right." The man crossed the room and sat down on the edge of his son's bed. "Why does the light hurt your eyes?"

"I don't know. I have a headache. It just does," Martin mumbled from beneath the sheet.

"Mrs. Cribbins said you were breaking out in some kind of rash. Do you want to show me?" Mr. Craven gently pulled the sheet away from the boy's face. His eyelids were swollen and red. Martin held his hand up over his face, as though even the sliver of light from the edge of the blind disturbed him. Then his father noticed the rash on the back of his hand. He brushed his finger over it.

"It looks like poison ivy."

"That's what it feels like," Martin replied, "poison ivy."

"Now where would you have gotten into that?"

"Maybe at the dump. Must have been in Cecil's garden. I probably touched it with my hand then rubbed it into my eyes."

"Hmm. All right, I'll have Mrs. Cribbins bring you some calamine lotion. But be sure you tell me if it gets any worse, particularly around your eyes. That's nothing to fool around with."

"Dad, can you bring up the calamine? Mrs. Cribbins is driving me crazy."

"I'll just have her leave it. You can put it on yourself."

"And no doctor."

"We'll see how it is tomorrow." Mr. Craven patted the boy's knee through the sheet and stood up. Mrs. Cribbins was waiting in the hall.

"Well?"

"It's only a mild rash."

"A mild rash?" The housekeeper said in a low voice, "Did you look at his eyes?"

"Ingrid, it's only poison ivy. Most of it's on his hand and there's only a touch around his eyes. It should clear up in a day or two if he doesn't start scratching it. I told him you'd bring up some calamine."

28

The housekeeper started for the stairs.

"And let him put it on himself. I told him he could."
Mrs. Cribbins bit her lip and hurried down the stairs. The
boy ought to be seen by a doctor, she thought. It could be
dangerous if it got into his eyes. She was tempted to call
Tony's father, but after the argument the night before,
she checked herself. Fifteen minutes later she returned to
Martin's room with the calamine lotion and his breakfast
tray.

"It's turning into a beautiful day. Don't you want the
blinds open just a bit?" Martin was lying rigidly with his
back to her.

"I don't want them opened at all."

"Well, here's your breakfast. You'll feel better once
you've got something warm in you." She waited for the boy
to sit up so she could prop the tray in his lap. "They're blue-
berry pancakes. And I smothered them in butter and maple
syrup, just the way you like them. Don't you want to eat
while they're still hot?" She tried to entice him, but when
he made no move to sit up, she set the tray on the night-
stand and reached for the cord to the lamp.

"Don't. The light hurts my eyes. Anyway, I don't need
it. I'm tired. I want to sleep some more."

"The calamine lotion is on your tray. You ought to use it
before you doze off again."

"Yes, I know, Mrs. Cribbins." The boy's voice had a
sassy edge that made the housekeeper cringe.

At a little past one, when Mr. Craven left the house,
Mrs. Cribbins looked in on Martin again. His breakfast was

untouched and he seemed to be sleeping. She quietly left the room, taking the tray with her.

*

It was growing dark when Nora left Maxine's house. The leaves crunched beneath her feet as she trudged across the lawn. The bough of an old tree creaked against the wind. The air was damp and chilly, and the dark sky threatened rain. Nora buried her hands in her pockets and hurried down the street.

A few blocks from home, she suddenly felt uneasy. The streets were deserted and the sky was pitch black. Except for the sound of her walking, everything seemed so still. Too still. There was something unnerving, she thought, about listening to your own footsteps. When Nora reached the corner of Willoughby and High streets, a second set of footsteps sounded somewhere behind her. She stopped and looked back. There was no one else on the sidewalk as far as she could see. When she turned the corner, the footsteps resumed, only now they came more quickly and seemed to be getting closer. Nervously, Nora crossed to the other side of the street and glanced back. The lights of a car suddenly bobbed over the hill, for a moment blinding her. Something leaped into the brush alongside the road as the car horn beeped in friendly recognition. It was Mr. Craven. Nora waved and glanced once back at the corner. She ran the last block home.

*

"How's Martin?" Mr. Craven asked, closing the front door behind him and slinging his jacket on the back of a chair.

"He's been sleeping all day and didn't touch his breakfast. Are you sure you don't want me to call Dr. Lane?"

"Let's see how Marty is at supper. I don't want to bring Mark over here for a case of poison ivy."

"The boy hasn't eaten anything since yesterday afternoon," Mrs. Cribbins persisted.

"Ingrid, it's not the first time he's lost his appetite. His stomach's probably still a little upset from yesterday. Has he complained of cramps again?"

"No, but . . ."

"Then stop worrying. Let the boy sleep and we'll see how he's feeling by supper."

But by suppertime Martin seemed unchanged.

"I'm not hungry," he mumbled from beneath the sheets when his father woke him.

"Marty, you haven't eaten anything since yesterday."

"All right. But can I have it up here?"

"Are you sure you're O.K.?" Mr. Craven started into the darkened room.

"Sure. I'm just tired."

"You've been sleeping all day."

"I'm O.K. I'll be all right tomorrow."

"I'll ask Mrs. Cribbins to fix you another tray. And please, try and eat something this time, would you?"

As soon as his father had left the tray and returned downstairs, Martin scooped most of his dinner into a napkin then slipped down the hall to the bathroom and disposed of it. An hour later, Mrs. Cribbins came up for the tray.

"Well, that's better," she remarked with satisfaction. "Do you want some more?"

"No." Martin's voice came hoarsely from under the covers. "I'm full."

*

Across the street, Nora turned restlessly in her bed. She awakened suddenly, with the vague memory of having had a bad dream, something about being followed. Down the hall, she could hear the refrigerator door close and water running in the sink. Someone else in the house was having trouble sleeping.

The shrubs outside tossed gently in the wind, their branches grazing her window pane. Nora gazed sleepily at the waving dark shapes, frondlike clumps of evergreen that cast shadows across the wall. The shadows reminded her of other things. A fluffy-headed dog, a large bird pecking at an oversized hand, the chiseled face of a man. The shadow figures swayed and bobbed, like silhouettes of passengers in a boat being rocked by the sea. Her ears pricked to a scratching sound that came from outside her window, barely audible but constant, as if a mouse were gnawing its way through a wall. Nora abruptly pulled herself up and flicked on the light by her bed. The sound stopped. Just a branch scraping against the glass, she thought, squinting across at the window. Without her glasses, she saw the evergreens blurred together into an indistinct mass. Nora reached for her glasses on the night table and started from her bed. The shrubs outside still swayed gently, in the light just an ordinary hedge. Nora crawled back into bed, turned off the light, and burrowed deep under the covers. The bird, the dog, and the hand resumed their dance on the wall. The shadow of the man's face had gone.

4

The Changeling

CLOSE TO THREE in the morning, Mrs. Cribbins suddenly awoke. A chilly breeze caressed the back of her neck and the room smelled musty, like mildew. Turning over, she saw Martin standing by her bed. Something glistened at the corners of his mouth. He was smiling.

The light from a street lamp filtered softly through the curtains, waving in the breeze behind him. Martin sat at the edge of the bed and leaned forward as if to whisper. Dulled by sleep, the housekeeper clumsily began to pull herself up. Abruptly, Martin pressed his lips to hers and exhaled deeply. Mrs. Cribbins's face tingled and grew numb. She felt as if she was drowning in icy waters. As the boy's breath reached her lungs, she was dimly aware of her body going limp and her head sagged back on the pillow. It was not the components of human breath, or life, that penetrated the tiny capillaries and scattered into her bloodstream. An alien awareness seemed to awaken behind her eyes, crowding her, pushing her back into some distant corner of her mind. She watched the room around her become suddenly bright, the air itself coming to life with dustlike particles of light. She felt as though she was seeing through the eyes of a night animal, a creature of prey.

Mrs. Cribbins wedged her tongue against the roof of her mouth, blocking the stream of icy breath. With one arm, she pushed Martin away. Her hand searched for the lamp by her bed and flicked it on. Martin hissed at the sudden flood of light and darted from the room. Leaning to the side of her bed, Mrs. Cribbins coughed violently. Her throat felt pricked with slivers of ice. Burning tears streamed from her eyes. Weakly, she pulled herself from the bed and groped her way through the hall. She heard Martin's door close in the darkness behind her.

"Hartford!" she cried, flicking on the hall light and banging at Mr. Craven's door. Groggily, the man opened it and squinted out at her.

"Martin! It's Martin!" She grasped the front of the man's nightshirt and pulled him into the hall.

"What's going on? It's three in the morning."

"I knew it! I knew the boy was hiding something!" she said breathlessly, tugging him toward the door at the end of the hall. Before he could stop her she'd flung the door open.

"What are you talking about? Why are you waking him?"

"He's not sleeping." The housekeeper's hands were shaking uncontrollably. Mr. Craven looked at her for a long moment, then entered the boy's room. Cold air poured in through the open window. He closed it and walked to the bed. The light from the hall cast a faint glow into the room. Martin's face was buried in his pillow. His breathing was shallow and regular. Mr. Craven looked back at the silhouette of the housekeeper in the doorway.

"He's sleeping," he whispered to her. Mrs. Cribbins stood rigidly outside the door.

"He's not. He's faking," she replied bitterly.

"Marty?" Mr. Craven shook the boy's shoulder lightly. Martin turned his head slightly to the side, revealing the traces of a rash, then curled his hand under his chin and moaned softly. Mr. Craven returned to the hall and closed the door.

"The boy's asleep, Ingrid."

"He can't be! He was just in my room!"

"Lower your voice," Mr. Craven whispered harshly, holding a finger to his lips.

"But the boy isn't sleeping! I told you . . ."

"Please," Mr. Craven pleaded, "come downstairs." The housekeeper followed him down to the den.

"It's an act." She paced the room in agitation. "I sensed something was wrong from the beginning." Mr. Craven poured each of them a glass of brandy, but the housekeeper left hers untouched on the table.

"Please, Ingrid, just tell me what happened."

Mrs. Cribbins shuddered. She searched her mind for

some way to describe what had happened. Slowly, she began. Mr. Craven paced as she spoke, then stopped and stared at her coldly.

"This is preposterous," he interrupted. "You were obviously having a nightmare."

"But there's more. Let me finish," the housekeeper pleaded.

"It was a dream," Mr. Craven said harshly. "And you're a fool to believe it was any more than that."

"It was not a dream!" The housekeeper's voice rose to meet his anger.

"Ingrid, I think you should drink that brandy and try to go back to bed."

"I will not sleep in this house till that boy is seen by a doctor. And a minister."

"A minister! I've heard enough. I'm going back to bed."

"Ask the boy. Bring him down here and ask him."

"I'll do no such thing. And neither will you. I forbid it. The boy's asleep. I'm not dragging him out of bed to terrify him with these absurd accusations."

The housekeeper was on the verge of tears. "You won't even talk to him?"

"No."

"Then I can't stay here."

"Suit yourself. But you're being very foolish." Mr. Craven put his glass down and left the room. The housekeeper sat in the same place till dawn, then went upstairs and packed.

*

Tony stood outside the Cravens' front gate waiting for Martin. The cold October wind whipped against his bare hands and face. He'd been waiting for ten minutes and was about to go and ring the bell, when a cab pulled up to the curb and the door to the Craven house opened.

"But this is absurd! Where will you go?" Mr. Craven's voice drifted over the yard. Several pigeons shot up from the lawn to the eaves of the old house. Tony tugged the sleeves of his sweater over his hands and buried them under his arms. He looked up through the gate, expecting to see Martin. Instead, Mrs. Cribbins came down the stairs, carrying a large suitcase. Feeling conspicuous and out of place, Tony slipped behind a hedge outside the gate.

"I'm sure I'll manage." The small woman put down her suitcase at the foot of the stairs, fished in her pocket, and handed her key to Mr. Craven, who made no move to take it.

"Please, Ingrid, the boy needs you."

"I told you what the boy needs. But you won't listen." Mrs. Cribbins set the key on the bottom step, picked up her suitcase, and started down the walk.

"Can't I reason with you?" Mr. Craven's voice quavered. His unshaven face looked ashen against the dark oak door. Without replying, Mrs. Cribbins continued out through the gate. She collided with Tony at the corner of the hedge. The housekeeper stiffened, her thin hand tightening its grip.

"I'm waiting for Marty," Tony explained with embarrassment. Mrs. Cribbins bit her lip and quickly glanced back at the man in the doorway.

"Martin is ill. You better go on to school," she said brusquely. Tony heard the door to the house close behind him. He gathered up his books from the sidewalk as Mrs. Cribbins hobbled to the curb and climbed into the waiting cab. Tony watched till it turned the corner, then glanced up the walk to the front of the house, unsure of what to do. He had always waited for Martin. Somehow it seemed disloyal, to go ahead alone. The icy wind prodded him from behind. Reluctantly, he walked on.

5

A Sickness of Light

Nora burst through the door, rain glistening in her matted curls, running down her neck and under her collar. She yanked the glasses from her nose, wiped them along her sleeve, and stuck them back on. Then she glared at her brother. Puddles were beginning to form around her feet.

"Well, are you going to tell me what's bugging you?" Tony pulled a rain-soaked sweater over his head. His voice came muffled through the wool. "You haven't said a word all the way home."

Nora ignored him and kicked off her shoes, which flopped like dead fish by the door.

"Hey, watch the mail!" Tony bent toward the scattered envelopes beneath the mail slot. Nora lunged and got to them first. She sorted through them while her brother looked on impatiently, then quickly stuffed a small yellow envelope into her hip pocket. She tossed the rest of the mail onto the hall table and walked away.

"Was that for me?" Tony started after her. "Nora, I asked you if that letter was for me?" Ignoring him, she hurried down the hall, her wool socks leaving damp prints on the dark wood floor. Reaching her bedroom, she quickly closed the door.

"Nora!" Tony called from the other side, knocking loudly. After a moment, he sighed and walked off toward the kitchen. Nora pulled the crumpled letter from her pocket. She looked at the yellow envelope with disgust; carefully lettered in orange ink, it was addressed to Anthony Lane. Nora tore open the flap and removed a folded card with a hand-drawn pumpkin on the front. If the pumpkin were real, Nora thought, she would kick in its grinning face. She read the message inside, then tossed the note angrily onto her bed.

A chair scraped across the floor above her. Then came the tapping of keys from her mother's typewriter. Nora made a face at the ceiling, pulled off her wet jeans, then her jersey, and dropped them in a heap on the floor. She took her terrycloth robe and dried her hair with one end. For a moment she stared at her reflection in the mirror on the back of the door. It wasn't fair, she thought, frowning at her flushed round face. It just wasn't fair. She slipped on the robe and crawled into bed. For a while, she just lay there, staring at the ceiling. Then she picked up the card and reread it. It just wasn't fair.

*

An hour later, Dr. Lane walked into the kitchen brushing the rain from his shoulders. He set his black bag on the counter.

"I visited your friend Martin today."

"What's the matter with him, Dad?" Tony looked up from his homework, strewn across the table.

"I'm not sure yet. Seems to be some form of phototoxicity. But I've run tests for every disease exhibiting sun-allergic symptoms. So far they've all come back negative."

"What's phototox . . ."

Dr. Lane smiled. "Phototoxicity? It's a condition in which a rash or some pain occurs when a person is exposed to sunlight. But Martin's even having these reactions to moderate electric light. Any light source makes him uncomfortable and produces a rash. And his pupils don't contract. That's what our eyes do under bright light so the light doesn't hurt them. The pupil regulates the amount of light that gets into the eye. Martin's stay dilated. He's also sensitive to heat. It's an odd group of symptoms. All we can do for the time being is keep him in a dark, cool room and run more tests."

"Dad, I want to know if Marty's going to be O.K.," Tony asked impatiently.

"It may take a little while, but we'll get him back in shape." Dr. Lane tousled his son's hair, attempting to break the serious mood. Tony brushed it back with embarrassment.

"Anyway, how are you doing? How was your day?"

Tony told him about Nora. He was pretty sure the letter had been for him.

"You're taking it pretty lightly." Dr. Lane regarded his son.

"The envelope was yellow." Tony smirked. "It was probably just from some girl."

"Yellow, huh. Was it scented, too?" Dr. Lane was smiling. Tony began to blush. "Aren't you even curious?"

"You know how Nora is when she's mad about something. I figured I'd let her cool off."

"Nora cool?" Dr. Lane laughed. "Don't hold your breath. Come on, let's talk to her."

*

Nora had dozed off. When she opened her eyes, her father was standing by the foot of her bed with his hand outstretched. Nora blinked up at him drowsily.

"I hear you might have something that belongs to your brother. Would you like it if he read your mail?"

"I never get any," Nora said, sulkily. Then she spotted Tony standing outside in the hall. She glared at him.

"Well? I'm waiting." Her father was still holding out his hand. Nora then realized that she was lying on top of the invitation. The envelope was with her clothes scattered at the foot of the bed. For a moment, she hesitated, then thought better of it and pulled it out from under her.

"I wish you would stop teasing your brother." Her father took the card and shook his head disapprovingly.

"Me?" Nora whined. "It's him! The whole thing's a

43

conspiracy!" She flopped over on her stomach and pouted. "Everyone's going except me!"

"Going where? What are you talking about?" Her father glanced down at the invitation.

"Audrey Quinn's having a Halloween party, and she invited everyone but me."

Tony stepped into the room and took the invitation from his father. As he looked at it, he frowned. "Oh, brother! So this is why you've been giving me the silent treatment all day. I should have guessed it."

"Guessed it my eye!" She said sulkily, "You knew about it all along. Everyone did!"

"Nora, really . . ." Tony began.

"I wouldn't be surprised if it was you who told Audrey not to ask me in the first place."

"Nora, quiet down! Your mother's trying to work." Dr. Lane looked helplessly from one child to the other.

"Look," Tony started, "I didn't know anything about this party till just now."

"It wasn't very nice of her only to ask one of you. It's rather immature. I wouldn't go."

Nora looked hopefully at her father.

"Of course," he went on, "it's Tony's choice."

"Are you going?" She pouted, making herself look as miserable as possible. Relishing his moment of power, Tony stood there silently and looked thoughtful.

"Well? Are you?" Nora was nearly begging. She knew Audrey had a crush on him. If he didn't go, it would be a small measure of triumph.

"All those girls ever want to do is dance. Boring, if you ask me." Tony dropped the invitation on Nora's bed and started from the room.

"Well, now what do you have to say?" Dr. Lane leveled his gaze at Nora. Reluctantly, she mumbled after her brother, "I'm sorry."

Tony turned at the door. He saw his sister as something comical. He would never dream of getting so worked up over the things that she did. But part of him felt sorry for her, too.

"What made you think I had anything to do with your not getting invited?"

"I've heard the kids talking about you and Audrey. I figured you just didn't want me around."

"Me and Audrey? Nora, I hardly even know her. You know that." Tony blushed at the idea that his friends might think he and Audrey had something going.

"Well, that's not what Audrey's been telling people."

"Unbelievable." Tony shook his head from side to side. "No way am I going to that party." Then he heard Nora giggle. "What's so funny?"

"You don't like Audrey any more than I do." Nora grinned.

"Don't *like* her? I can't *stand* her." Tony frowned, then, catching the twinkle in Nora's eye, could not help grinning back.

*

After dinner, Maxine called Nora to say she wasn't going to the party either.

"But I thought you got invited?"

"I did," Maxine replied. "I just said I wasn't going."

"Has everyone gone crazy around here? I'd give my right arm to go to that party."

"Nora, sometimes you really are dense."

"And what's that supposed to mean?" Nora asked defensively.

"Look, if Audrey invited everyone but me to her party, would you go?"

Nora was silent for a moment. "No, I guess not. Not if you weren't going to be there. Darn it, Max, this whole thing burns me up."

"I know. Hey, I meant to ask, do you know what's wrong with Marty?"

"Dad said he has some kind of allergy," Nora replied without interest.

"Is that all? My mother ran into Mrs. Cribbins today. She said the way the old lady carried on, you'd think Marty was on his deathbed. She moved out, you know."

"Yeah, I know. Dad told us. Look, Max, about the party . . ."

"Forget it. We'll figure out something better to do."

"I didn't mean that. I just wanted to say, well, you know."

"I know. See you tomorrow." After hanging up, Maxine picked up the invitation lying on her desk. It was the first masquerade party she'd ever been invited to. "Well, easy come, easy go," she said to herself, tearing the invitation in half and dropping it into the wastebasket.

On the other side of town, Mrs. Cribbins was settling in to the small apartment she rented above Sweeney's Hardware Store. Her suitcase was open on the bed.

"Mrs. Cribbins?" Mr. Sweeney knocked at the door. "There's a call for you downstairs."

"Who'd be calling me?" she asked, opening the door.

"I didn't ask who it was." The small baldheaded man preceded her down the stairs. The housekeeper picked the phone up from the counter.

"Hello? Ingrid Cribbins speaking."

The voice at the other end was strangely harsh, almost as though it was inhaling with each word. The sound was like that of someone suffocating. The words were barely intelligible.

"Who is this?" the housekeeper asked gravely. After a moment, a familiar voice came over the wire.

"Ingrid, please come back," Hartford Craven pleaded. "He needs you."

"Was that the boy?" Sweat broke out over Mrs. Cribbins's forehead.

"Please Ingrid, for Martin's sake."

"I told you what he needs," Mrs. Cribbins said coldly. "There's nothing more I can do."

"But he wants you. Please, Ingrid. At least talk to him." There was a silence. Then Martin's voice, again sounding harsh and muffled.

"Inga," he called her by the affectionate name he had

used when she first came to take care of him. Mrs. Cribbins began to sob, silently, covering the mouthpiece with her hand.

"Come back, Inga, I need you."

Mrs. Cribbins laid the phone gently back in its cradle. "It isn't Martin," she said aloud, as if to convince herself. "It isn't. It isn't him."

6

The Visit

THE SKY WAS overcast with great swirling clouds that threatened to burst open at any moment. Maxine and Nora were walking quickly to beat the rain. Just as they stepped in the door, it began to pour.

"That was close." Maxine left her jacket and books in the hall and followed Nora into the living room. Nora nestled into one corner of the window seat, tucking her knees under her chin.

"Still mad about Audrey?" Maxine squatted awkwardly in the other end of the window seat, her long legs folding up like a grasshopper's. Nora nodded, staring moodily out across the street. The Craven house loomed out of the mist and rain like some great ship washed ashore. Pigeons clustered under the eaves and along the window sills. Both girls watched the old house in silence.

The sky grew darker. A street lamp blinked on, casting its hooded light over the glistening pavement. Nikki, the Cravens' black angora, emerged from the garage at the side of the house.

"He looks a lot bigger than I remember," Maxine remarked. Nora nodded. "I thought cats hated the rain."

"Maybe they don't know he's out there." The cat prowled through the hedges that grew alongside the drive, then sprinted through the gate and across the street.

"Look, Nora, he's coming over here. Maybe we should let him in." The cat crept into the Lanes' front yard. It sat in the walkway, its black fur sleek with rain, and began to lick its paw. Nora disliked the cat; she wanted to shoo it away. Nikki suddenly looked up at the window where the girls were sitting. He stood and stretched, then slowly walked toward the door. The animal's tail, matted from the rain and slender as a snake, twitched nervously.

"Let's bring him in." Maxine jumped up and moved quickly toward the door.

"Don't! I hate that cat," Nora shouted, a moment too late. Nikki stepped cautiously through the door. When Maxine reached out to pick him up, he darted through the hall into the living room, keeping himself in the shadows. He kept his eyes on Nora.

"Here, kitty." Maxine followed him into the room. Nikki slid behind a chair and crouched. Maxine got to her knees and stretched her hand out to the cat. When her fingers touched its thick black coat, the cat hissed and swiped her with its claw. Maxine jerked her hand back.

"Why did he do that? I was only going to pet him." She inspected the scratch on her wrist.

"I told you he was awful." Nora jumped from her seat to chase Nikki back outside. "Go on! Get out of here!" She was about to nudge the cat with her foot when it darted back into the hall and up the stairs. "Now look what you've done." Nora frowned. "And he sheds that awful fur everywhere."

Maxine followed Nora up the stairs. From the end of the hall, the muffled tapping of Mrs. Lane's typewriter sounded behind a closed door. Nora looked in her parents' bedroom. The cat was not there. They checked the bathroom and the linen closet.

"What are you doing?" Tony appeared at the top of the stairs.

"Cravens' cat ran up here. We're trying to find it," Maxine answered.

"How'd he get in?"

"I let him in. It was raining."

"Well, he's a sneaky one. Good luck." Tony stepped into his room and closed the door.

"Now where?" Maxine asked.

"There's nowhere else." Nora grinned mischievously.

"But it has to be up here somewhere."

"It is. It's in Tony's room."

"Well, shouldn't we tell him?"

"He'll find out soon enough." Nora smiled and started back downstairs. After all, she thought, Tony always wanted a cat.

*

An hour later, Nora's mother went to the door to meet her husband.

"Smells good. What's for dinner?"

Mrs. Lane took his coat and hung it in the closet. When she turned her husband wrapped his arms around her.

"Meatloaf. And don't say anything. It could have been hamburgers again." She disentangled herself and put his black bag under the hall table. "Did you see Martin Craven today?"

Dr. Lane nodded. "No change. We still don't know what it is."

"Oh no."

"And it's taking its toll on Hartford. I wish I could talk Ingrid Cribbins into going back. I don't think the man is eating."

"Why did she leave them, anyway? Doesn't anyone know?"

"They had a row over something. But neither of them wants to talk about it."

"What about Martin? I hope, at least, that Hartford's feeding *him* properly."

"I'm afraid Martin doesn't have much of an appetite. He sleeps most of the day. When I went in to examine him, I had his father try to feed him some soup. The boy wouldn't touch it."

"That poor man. I'll send Tony over with something hot after supper."

"It's a good idea. He could use it." Dr. Lane followed his wife to the kitchen.

*

After dinner, Tony took a platter of food over to the Cravens. He sat in Martin's room, hunched forward in his chair. A cold breeze blew in through a partially opened window. Tony pulled his jacket tighter. Mr. Craven sat beside him.

Except for the moonlight filtering through the curtains, the room was in darkness. Tony could not see his friend's face, which was pressed into the pillow. Martin's hands clutched at the sheets like claws, his fingers digging into the mattress. After a moment, Mr. Craven stood to leave.

"He's been like this all day," the man whispered. "Maybe if you come back tomorrow . . ."

"Is it all right if I sit a little longer? Maybe he'll wake up."

"Of course." Mr. Craven patted him on the shoulder. "I have to catch up on some work, Tony. Do you mind letting yourself out?"

Tony nodded and looked back to the bed. Mr. Craven left the room and closed the door softly behind him. When the man's footsteps faded on the stairs, Martin suddenly turned over.

"Are you awake?" Tony whispered. As he leaned forward in his seat it seemed that his friend was smiling.

"Tony." Martin's voice sounded strangely harsh, as though he was sucking at the air. Saliva trickled from the corners of his mouth.

"Your dad was just here. We thought you were sleeping."

"I can't see you. Come closer," Martin's voice whispered hoarsely.

"Should I turn on the light?" Tony reached toward the lamp on the night table.

"Don't." Martin pulled himself up. "It hurts my eyes. Come here, sit on the bed." Tony dutifully moved from the chair and sat at the foot of the bed.

"Dad said you had some sort of allergy. Does it hurt?"

Martin giggled.

"What's funny?"

"I'm not sick." Martin leaned toward him.

"What are you talking about? What about the rash?"

"There isn't any."

"Then why are you staying in bed?"

"It's a secret."

"Tell me, Marty."

"I can't."

"Why? Are you worried I'll tell your dad?"

"I can't tell you. But I can show you."

"I don't understand."

"Do you really want to know?"

"Of course I do." Tony shifted uneasily.

"Then lie down here next to me. It's all right. Come on."

Tony peered through the darkness at the shadow of his friend's face.

"Come on," Martin coaxed him. "Don't be afraid."

"I'm not afraid. I just don't see what difference it makes whether I'm lying or sitting."

"It does. If you don't lie down, I can't show you."

"Marty, I don't know." Tony hesitated.

"You're afraid." Martin turned away from him, appearing to brood.

"Oh, all right." Tony stretched out stiffly on his back. "Well?"

Martin threw an arm across his friend's chest and jumped on top of him, pinning Tony's arms by his sides.

"Marty, what are you doing?" Tony shifted uncomfortably beneath the boy's weight. Martin's pungent breath poured like a river of ice over his face. Tony tried to turn his head away. Martin jammed his knees into the boy's ribs and grasped the sides of his head, forcing his face upward. Then Tony saw his friend's eyes and shuddered. Martin's pupils were grotesquely enlarged, crowding out the whites. At the corners of his mouth a dark substance glistened. Tony struggled to break away. Martin clamped his mouth against Tony's and exhaled deeply. A numbing sensation seeped over Tony's face, spreading down his throat and into his lungs. His legs continued to thrash. He had a dim sense of drowning, and tried to hold his breath, but as exertion overcame him, he sucked in deeply. Gradually his thoughts dispersed like foam on the crest of a breaking wave. Then the darkness ebbed away. Everything in the room began to pulse with its own light and color. Even the air burst into a swirling phosphorescent mist. Through the window, the street lamp outside no longer cast its familiar gentle light, but burned furiously, throwing out waves of heat that seared the boy's eyes and pricked his skin. Voices echoed inside of him, not voices really, but rhythms, humming through his veins and urging him out to the welcoming night.

7

The Nightmare

WHILE TONY WAS with Martin, Nora had fallen asleep in the window seat. She was dreaming that something was chasing her through the cold night. A street lamp glowed warmly in her dream, casting a disc of light onto the pavement. She knew she would be safe in the light. She ran barefoot over the wet grass. As the thing stalking her drew near, the air grew foul and filled with the smell of decay. She stumbled. A dead cat lay at her feet. It was covered with fireflies. She held her hands out over it for warmth, but the flies stung her fingers. As she held up her hands, the wounds bled, and the blood glistened with tiny particles of ice.

"I've been looking for you," a familiar voice called out from the darkness above. Nora tried to crawl away.

"Come on. Get up," the voice ordered. It was a woman's voice, but when she looked up she saw that it came from a dark brooding figure the size of a boy. When he bent his face closer, she saw that his eyes were entirely black and grotesquely enlarged, like an insect's.

"Get up. Come on, get up." Icy fingers slid over her face, then pulled her from the ground. Nora struggled, away from the hands, up through suffocating sleep.

"Darling, get up."

Nora blinked open her eyes. The familiar warmth in her mother's voice was as comforting as an embrace. Nora inhaled deeply, trembling. Her mother was smoothing the hair back from her forehead.

"Why were you sleeping out here?" Mrs. Lane wrapped a warm, protective arm around her as she sat next to Nora in the seat.

"I was waiting for Tony to come home. I had this awful nightmare," Nora shuddered. Her mother pulled her closer.

"I know. That's how I found you. You called for him in your sleep."

"I did?" Nora asked, not recalling his presence in her dream. "Is he back yet, Mom?" Now she wondered how long she'd been sleeping.

"Not yet. I'm sure he'll be along soon, though."

"Where's Dad?"

"In bed. And that's right where you're going, too." Mrs. Lane eased Nora up, and with one arm around her, led her to her room. Nora changed to her nightgown and crawled into bed. Then her mother kissed her forehead and turned out the light.

"Mom, leave the door open a crack."

Nora looked gratefully at the shape of her mother, tall and comforting, silhouetted against the hall light. "I just want to hear when Tony comes in."

"Want to be sure we're all on board before you sail off to sleep?"

Nora could tell from her mother's voice that she was smiling.

" 'Night, Mom." Nora drew the sheet up beneath her eyes, afraid to close them. She hadn't been so disturbed by a dream since she was a small child. Then she shared a room with Tony, and they both had many nightmares. It was funny, she thought, how when she used to have bad dreams, Tony would usually have them too. They weren't often the same dreams, but they were always similar. Her father used to say it was because they slept in the same room. But Nora always believed it was because they were twins, and also, that they were so close then, back when they were small. She tried to think of other things, of Halloween, and school and Maxine. But the dream kept weaving through her thoughts. She couldn't shake it.

Her eyes fastened on the warm bright light that spilled through her door. For an instant she closed them. Two enormous icy black eyes stared coldly into her mind. She curled on her side and gazed back at the comforting light from the hall. After a while, she began to doze.

*

The front door opened and closed, the lock turned, and the hall light went out. Nora sat bolt upright in her bed. Footsteps moved softly down the hall. Nora slid from her bed and crept to the door.

"Tony? Is that you?" When there was no answer, Nora stepped into the hall. Her brother was halfway up the stairs. He moved like a somnambulist, she thought, as if he were in a trance, with one hand on the railing.

"Tony?" she called again. Her brother continued upward, unhearing. He stopped at the top of the stairs. For a moment he just stood there, as if he were trying to remember something. Nora flicked on the hall light. Her brother's hand rushed to cover his eyes.

"Turn it out."

"Are you O.K.?" Nora asked.

Tony stepped back into the hall. His free hand brushed over the wall till it found the door to his room. He quickly stepped inside and closed it. Nora frowned, shrugged, then started back to her room. It took a long time for her to sleep again, and when she did, she slept fitfully.

*

"Where's Tony?" Nora asked, piling her books on the breakfast table. Dr. Lane had already gone to his office. Her mother was standing over the waffle iron, gazing out the window at the morning rain. A sheet of vapor hovered over the brook that ran through the back yard.

"He doesn't feel well. It's probably just a cold. But I'm keeping him home to be on the safe side."

Nora started to rise from her chair.

"Better not go up, dear. I don't want you catching it too."

"But I have to ask him something."

"I think he's trying to sleep. Won't it keep till after school?"

Nora looked down at the plate of waffles her mother had just set in front of her. A pat of butter melted beneath the syrup. She sniffed the steamy amber sweetness and sat back down. Nora picked up her fork and ate quickly, gulping great mouthfuls and washing them down with orange juice.

"What's your hurry?" Mrs. Lane was just sitting down across from her.

"I've got something to do before I go to school."

When she finished, Nora gathered her books and ran back to her room. She tore a piece of paper from her notebook and quickly jotted across it:

"It means a lot to me that you and Max aren't going to the party. I was thinking, if Marty's better by then, maybe the four of us could have a little party of our own." She folded it in half and scrawled across the top: "Tony." She ran upstairs and slipped the note under her brother's door. Then she put on her coat, grabbed her books, and left for school.

Outside, her breath turned white as it hit the damp cool air. Halfway down the block, she felt a prickling sensation at the back of her neck, as if she were being watched. She stopped and glanced back at the house. Through the drizzle, she could vaguely make out a black spot between the curtains and the window of her brother's room. It was Nikki, staring down at her. She'd forgotten all about the cat. It must have been hiding all night or Tony would have noticed it. Nora wanted to rush back and chase the animal out, but there wasn't time. She hurried on, silently scolding herself for not telling her brother the cat was up there in the first place. Well, she thought, the worst it could do was pee on the rug. She'd take care of it when she got home.

*

Maxine was waiting for her as she always did on the bench in front of school. Nora swooped down on her, eagerly telling Maxine her plan for Halloween.

"We could make all kinds of neat things to eat, and I'm sure there'll be a good horror movie on T.V. The four of us could sit around and give each other goosebumps."

"Great idea! Say, where is Tony?"

"He has a cold."

"Did he tell you how Marty was doing?"

"I didn't get a chance to ask him." Suddenly Nora began to feel uneasy. A picture was forming in her mind of the way Tony looked the night before. She remembered how he moved, as if he were sleepwalking, and the funny way he covered his eyes when the lights came on.

"What's the matter?" Maxine asked, noting the sudden change in Nora's face.

"Nothing. I was just thinking about a dream I had last night." Her dream, she thought, that was it. The way he looked in the dark hall, slowly climbing the stairs. It reminded her of the boy in her dream. "I'm getting cold, Max. Let's go inside."

8

In the Month of Worms

THE DAYS WERE growing shorter. Although school had only been out a half hour, the street lights were already on. October, Nora decided, was the month of worms. They were everywhere, bloated and floating in puddles along the sidewalks, in the gutters and in the grass. Nora walked slowly back from school. She was trying to avoid stepping on them. As she turned down Willoughby Street, she remembered the cat in Tony's room. She ran the last block home, wondering if he'd already been found. She banged the front door behind her.

"Don't drip all over the hall!" her mother shouted from the kitchen. Mrs. Lane was sitting over a cup of coffee and the evening crossword puzzle. "What's a seven-letter word for the Mountain of Muses from Greek mythology?" she asked as Nora walked into the kitchen.

"I don't know."

"Don't they teach you about those things in school?" Mrs. Lane nibbled the eraser.

"Ancient Greek? Mom, I'm only in eighth grade!"

"Well, it never hurts to ask. How about a seven-letter word for a bear in hibernation?"

"You got me. How's Tony feeling?"

"Like a bear in hibernation." Her mother scribbled the letters into the little boxes, "Grouchy!"

"Why? What's the matter?"

"I don't know. I'm waiting for your father to come home and take a look at him. Tony won't let me put his light on. Says it hurts his eyes. He doesn't have a fever, but he complains his room's too hot. Then he insisted I open his window. He's too hot, and I'm so cold I have two sweaters on and spent the day sitting down here by the stove. Want some cocoa?" Mrs. Lane folded up the paper.

"In a minute. I'll be right back." Nora brought her books to her room and then ran upstairs. Her brother's door was partially open. The curtains were drawn and the lights were out. Nora stepped inside. An odd sound came from Tony's bed. Vaguely, she could make out the form of the Cravens' cat, crouched on Tony's chest and purring loudly.

"Out, Nikki." Nora waved her hand at the animal. It turned its head, a low growl rising from its throat.

"Bad cat." Nora swatted at its tail. The cat hissed, leaping behind the curtains. A cold breeze made Nora shudder. She walked across the room to the window. When she parted the curtain, a paw swiped at her hand. In reflex, Nora swatted back at the bulge behind the drapes. But her hand met only air. She looked out the window. The cat, standing on the ground below, looked up at her, licking its paw.

"What are you doing?" Tony's voice came hoarsely out of the dark.

"I just found Nikki in here. He jumped out the window. I was just going to close it."

"Leave it open," Tony said flatly. Nora let the curtain fall back in place.

"Did you get my note?" she asked, but Tony turned away from her, burying his face in the pillow. As Nora's eyes adjusted to the dark, she noticed the blankets kicked in a heap at the foot of the bed. A tray of food sat untouched on the night stand. As she turned toward the door, she spotted the note she'd left for Tony that morning. It had been kicked beneath the rug with only one white corner poking over the doorsill. She stooped to pick it up.

"Close the door," Tony called harshly from behind her. She crumpled the note in her hand, closed the door, and returned downstairs.

*

"Something wrong?" Mrs. Lane put a cup of steaming chocolate in front of Nora.

"What?" Nora blinked and looked up.

"Why the long face?"

"I just went up to see Tony." Nora hesitated, unsure how to explain what she felt.

"Is he awake?"

Nora nodded. Her mother returned to the stove and poured a second cup of cocoa.

"I'll be right back. I want to check in on him." Mrs. Lane carried the other mug of chocolate up to Tony's room. As she opened the door she was met by a chilly breeze. The curtains swayed in the window. The light from the hall beamed through the doorway and over the bed.

"Close it," Tony said harshly, drawing the sheets up over his head. His mother pushed the door shut with her foot.

"I brought you some hot chocolate." She set the cup beside the other food on the night stand and sat on the edge of his bed. Leaning forward she placed the back of her hand against Tony's cheek. It felt like ice. The boy moaned uncomfortably, pushing her hand away. Mrs. Lane sat still for a moment, looking down at him through the darkness. She saw a moist spot glistening faintly where his mouth had been pressed to the pillow.

"This isn't just a cold," she said aloud to herself. Tony turned toward his mother. He pulled himself up till his face was level with hers. She could feel his cold breath on her face. In the dark, beneath swollen eyelids his eyes shimmered like deep black pools. Although they looked directly at her, they seemed somehow vacant. Then she noticed that he was smiling. But it was not the gentle, boyish smile of her son. Mrs. Lane stood quickly and walked to the door.

"Try to drink some of that cocoa," she said, stepping out to the hall. "Your father will be up as soon as he comes home."

*

When Dr. Lane came in, his wife rushed out to the hall to meet him. "I'm worried about Tony. He's been home in bed all day. I thought he was just coming down with a cold, but now I'm not so sure. I can't get him to eat anything, and he's been complaining that the light hurts his eyes."

Dr. Lane was hanging up his coat. He stopped and turned.

"His eyes hurt? Is he also feeling hot?"

"Yes, but his skin feels like ice. He insists the room's too stuffy and he asked me to leave his window open. I've tried to close it twice but as soon as I leave the room he opens it again."

"When you turned on the light, did you notice a rash, or whether his pupils were dilated?"

"I don't know. His room's been kept dark all day. He slept till about half an hour ago."

Dr. Lane picked up his black bag and ascended the stairs. He looked worried.

"Shall I come with you?" Mrs. Lane looked up at her husband.

"No. Better not. Sounds like the same thing the Craven boy has. And if it is, the examination is going to be unpleasant."

"Why?" his wife asked anxiously.

"Because of the light." Dr. Lane continued up the stairs and entered Tony's room. When the light came on, Tony's shouts could be heard all through the house.

"What's going on, Mom?" Nora ran out to the hall. Her

mother was standing at the bottom of the stairs, gripping the banister.

"Your father's examining Tony."

"But why's Tony shouting?"

"I don't know, dear." Mother and daughter stood silently in the hall, waiting. Soon after, Dr. Lane appeared at the top of the stairs.

"Janet, call the hospital and tell them I'm bringing him in. I want him in a private room. Be sure they have one available."

Mrs. Lane's face went white.

"It's all right. I just want to bring him in for some tests. I don't have everything I need here."

"What is it?" Mrs. Lane's voice was taut with worry.

"Looks like the same thing Martin has. Doesn't make any sense, though. An allergy wouldn't be contagious."

"How . . . how is the Craven boy?" she asked.

"We'll talk about it in the car. Call the hospital while I get him ready."

After she called the hospital, Dr. Lane had her go out and start up the car. When he carried the boy downstairs, Nora guessed why. He must not have wanted her mother upset by what she would have seen. Dr. Lane had Tony wrapped in a blanket. Even his head was covered. Tony was squirming, trying to push his way out of it. When they came to the foot of the stairs, the cover came loose and fell from his face. The boy moaned beneath the hall light, struggling to free his hands. Nora sucked in her breath.

Her brother's eyelids were swollen, as if the eyes themselves were pushing their way out of the sockets. The pupils were enlarged and his eyes darted wildly, blindly. His breathing was deep and harsh. It sounded as if he was suffocating. But most frightening, Nora observed, flattening herself in the shadow beneath the staircase so that she wouldn't be seen, was the effect of the light on Tony's skin. The moment the cover had fallen from her brother's face, a blistering rash began to appear. In the short time it took for her father to carry the boy from the stairs to the door, his smooth pale complexion had erupted into an angry red mask, as if he'd been burned by the light.

The moment they stepped out into the cold October night, the struggle subsided, Tony's breathing returned to normal, his body grew limp. Dr. Lane climbed into the back seat with the boy. Then his wife backed the car out of the driveway.

As the headlights turned into the street, a howl ripped through the darkness. The Cravens' cat stood in the middle of the road, caught in the glare of the headlights. Mrs. Lane, in her panic, must not have seen it. She accelerated and the car jumped forward. Nora shuddered. The car sped away. In the red glow of the tail lights, a dark furry shape lay lifeless in a swelling black pool.

Nora started from the step to inspect the dead cat. Somewhere in the night someone screamed. Through a window in the house across the street, she could see Mr. Craven running up the stairs. Wrapping her arms across her chest, Nora walked quickly out to the street.

She regarded the cat with morbid curiosity. The animal's

back had been crushed. The blood seeping from its body into the pavement seemed to glisten with tiny luminous particles. Nora shivered in the wind. Although the scene repulsed her, at the same time she felt drawn to it. For some reason she could not stop staring down into the dead cat's eyes. As she nudged it with her foot something pricked her toe. It was so slight she barely noticed it. But when she withdrew her foot the cat moved toward her. In horror, she realized the cat's claw had somehow gotten hooked into the fabric of her shoe. Frantically, she shook it free. When the body flopped back to the pavement, a dense luminous dust swirled out of the cat and drifted up on the wind. Nora's mouth dropped open. She ran back to the house and locked the door behind her.

*

Tony seemed to sleep on the short ride to the hospital, his head resting in his father's lap and his eyes closed. Dr. Lane put his hand to the boy's cheek. The rash had vanished as quickly as it had appeared, and in the dark interior of the car, his skin again grew cold as ice.

"I'll turn the heat on." Tony's mother fumbled beneath the dashboard. Dr. Lane glanced down at his son. Tony's eyes blinked open. His lips began to curl into a sneer.

"Better not, Janet. The heat bothers him."

Tony's eyes closed again, but his lips remained parted over glistening teeth.

*

At the hospital, Dr. Lane lifted Tony from the seat, being careful to shield the boy's face from any light. He bent to the window by the driver's seat. Tony's hooded face was pressed under his chin.

"Go on home. I can get a cab back."

Mrs. Lane already had the key out of the ignition.

"I can wait."

"But there's no reason to. He'll be O.K., Janet, I promise. Anyway, one of us ought to be home with Nora."

Reluctantly, she started the car and pulled away. Through the rearview mirror, she watched the attendants roll a cot out from the emergency room. As they strapped the boy in, the cover was pulled from his face. But by then she was too far away to hear the strange growl emerge from her son's throat or to see the odd rash appear on his face as the cot was rolled into the brightly lit corridor.

*

At home, Nora sat hunched in the window seat waiting for her parents to return. Nikki's dark shape lay lifeless in the middle of the road. In awe, she watched as wisps of glowing dust continued to curl above the cat. Feeling suddenly chilled, she went to her room for a sweater. While rummaging through her dresser, she heard a car turning down the street. Nora ran to the door, unlocked it, and darted out to the driveway as her mother's car pulled in.

"Where's Dad?"

"He's still at the hospital with Tony."

"Mom, I have to show you something." Nora began to tug at her mother's sleeve.

"It's freezing out here, Nora. And you don't even have a jacket on." Nora continued to pull her mother toward the street.

"What is it?" Mrs. Lane asked impatiently, pulling her arm free.

"The Cravens' cat. You ran over it."

"Oh no!" Her hand flew to her mouth. "Where is it?"

Nora pointed toward the street. "I went out to look right after you hit it. Its back was all crushed in. And some funny glowing stuff keeps pouring out of it."

"This is terrible." Nora's mother walked out to the road, not hearing. Nora followed close behind.

"Where did you say it was?"

Nora peered around her mother. Where the cat had been, there was only a large dark spot staining the road.

"It *was* there just a minute ago," Nora said incredulously.

"It must have crawled away."

"It *couldn't* have. Its back was all crushed, Mom. It couldn't have crawled an inch." Nora followed her mother from one side of the street to the other. "I don't get it. I'm sure it was dead. And that weird dust kept streaming out of it."

"Please, Nora, stop it." Her mother was growing agitated. "It *must* have crawled away." She glanced across at the Craven house. "I'll have to go in and call him. That poor man, this is the last thing he needs. I just hope it isn't hurt too badly."

"But Mom, I told you . . ."

"Nora, either help me look for it, or go back in the house!" Mrs. Lane interrupted impatiently.

"But he's dead, Mom. I saw him. And that funny glowing stuff . . ."

"If he's dead he'd still be here!" her mother said sharply. "And this glowing business . . . Nora, you're babbling nonsense."

Nora fell silent.

"Now go into the house and get me a flashlight. Maybe it's not too late to get it to a vet."

Nora ran back to the house. When she returned with the flashlight, her mother began to search the yard. As Nora looked up at the Craven house, she could just make out a silhouette of someone looking down from a second-floor window. Then the curtains closed. After a while her mother gave up and Nora followed her back to the house. Mrs. Lane called Martin's father.

"It's Janet, Hartford. I feel just terrible about this. I don't know how it could have happened. It seems I've hit Nikki." She paused briefly, then went on, "He's crawled away somewhere. I've looked in both our yards but I can't find a trace of him."

Nora shook her head and sighed, "Mom, I told you, he *couldn't* have crawled away."

"Shh." Her mother cut her off and spoke into the phone, "Nora saw it happen. Tony's ill. We were rushing him to the hospital. Unfortunately, I didn't even know about it till I got back home. I'm so sorry." She paused again. "I'll come out and look with you. He can't have gone too far." Silence, then, "No, I insist. It's the least I can do. I'll be over in just a few minutes." After hanging up, Nora immediately started in again.

"Mom, his back was all crushed in and that glowing stuff . . ."

"Nora, please," her mother interrupted, "you're not making any sense. There's an injured animal out there somewhere . . ."

"But Mom . . ."

"Not now. I've got to find Nikki." Her mother turned abruptly and left the house.

9

The Prowler

THE NEXT DAY, Nora met Maxine on the bench in front of school.

"Maybe it was just a patch of fog. And how can you be sure the cat didn't crawl away? He might have, when you weren't looking."

"He didn't crawl away," Nora replied with obvious exasperation. "I told you, he was dead."

"It sounds like a ghost story. 'The Cat That Vanished in a Puff of Smoke.'"

"Max," Nora said impatiently, "I didn't say he vanished in a puff of smoke. I just said that stuff was coming out of him, and that he was too dead to budge an inch. Don't you believe me?"

"I don't know, Nora. It just all sounds so strange."

"But it's true!" Nora said urgently. "I saw it as clearly as I see you now!"

Maxine pulled the collar up on her coat and looked across the yard.

"I can't stand it!" Nora suddenly stood. "Why does everyone think I'm lying?"

"Come on." Maxine grabbed her friend by the wrist. "It's not that I think you're lying, it's just that things might have happened a little differently than you think they did."

"Mr. Craven and my mother looked all over for Nikki this morning. They still couldn't find him."

"Maybe he just ran away. Animals do that when they're hurt. They get scared."

"Nikki was dead," Nora said flatly. "How many times do I have to tell you? His back was all crushed. There's a blood stain two feet wide smack in the middle of the road. And even if I was wrong and he wasn't dead, he still couldn't have gone very far."

"It's awful, what happened to Nikki." Maxine sighed. "But since no one's been able to find him, maybe you should just try to forget about it."

"I can't forget about it. I have a feeling something's going on, something . . . something weird."

"What are you talking about?"

"Everything!" Nora was exasperated. "This thing with the Cravens' cat. Those dead gulls Mom and I saw. And now Tony's sick, the way Marty is. I don't know how to explain it any better. It's just a feeling I have, that something isn't right."

"Have you talked to your Dad about it?"

"I tried." Nora shrugged. "He said I was having a nervous reaction to all these things happening at once. That's his way of saying it's all in my imagination."

"Did he tell you anything about Tony?"

"Just that he's still running tests. They have to keep him in a dark room; otherwise his eyes hurt and his skin breaks out in sores."

"It sounds awful."

"It is awful." Both girls sat silently, waiting for the bell to ring.

Once inside, Nora found herself staring at Tony's vacant seat. But Tony and Martin were not the only ones absent. There was a third empty desk at the back of the room. Peter Wade was out sick that day, too.

*

Tony's condition did not improve. Over the next three days, Nora's mother spent most of her time sitting by Tony's bed at the hospital. Sunday night, the Lanes ate supper early, then Nora's parents left to visit Tony. It was not a pleasant visit. Something seemed to change in Tony at nightfall. During the day, he had just slept in the dark air-conditioned hospital room. But when his parents came in, he became restless, pacing and staring out the window. His room was on the ground floor, at the back of the building, and the window looked out over a small woods. Outside, it was raining.

Dr. and Mrs. Lane shook out their coats and hung them on the back of his door to dry. Mrs. Lane went to kiss him, but Tony turned his head away. When they spoke to him, he only stared distractedly out at the dark woods.

*

At home, Nora had just finished studying and was beginning to undress for bed. As she slipped on her robe, something tapped at her window. Just outside a naked branch nodded in the wind. Rain beaded down the glass pane. Nora knotted her belt, then went to pull down the blind. The dark contour of the bushes that hugged the house was visible through her reflection. Suddenly they parted as something darted away. Nora released the blind and pressed her face to the window. Her breath caught. Deep footprints were imbedded in the mud outside. She jerked the blind down, then walked quickly out to the hall. Whoever it was, she thought anxiously, would have seen her parents drive away and know that she was alone.

Nora rushed to the kitchen to make sure the back door was locked. Then she ran to the front door and fastened the chain. She debated whether or not to call her parents at the hospital. What if they thought she was imagining things again? Finally, she picked up the phone. A list of emergency numbers was taped to the handle. Nora dialed the police.

A gruff voice answered. "Sergeant Wade, Precinct One, Covendale."

"This is Nora Lane. I live at thirteen Willoughby Street and there's someone looking in the windows."

"Nora Lane?" The gruff voice softened. "You're in school with my two kids, Peter and Karen, aren't you?"

"Yes," Nora answered. Her hand was shaking. "Mr. Wade, I'm scared."

"Where are your parents?"

"At the hospital, visiting my brother. Whoever's out there must have seen them go."

"All right. Just stay put. Are the doors locked?"

"Yes." Nora's voice was trembling.

"I'll send two of my men right over. Hold on." Nora could hear the man giving instructions over a crackling intercom to a patrol car. "You live across from the Cravens, don't you?"

"Yes sir," Nora answered.

"O.K. Nora, there's a car on the way. Until it gets there, I want you to check the ground floor windows and be sure they're all locked. Do you know if Mr. Craven is at home?"

"I don't know."

"After you check the windows, call him. If he is, ask if he'd just keep an eye out his window until the patrol car gets there. He may even offer to come over there and wait with you."

"Yes sir."

"All right. Remember, check the windows first. And try not to worry. It's probably just one of the neighborhood kids trying to give you a scare. Happens a lot around Halloween."

As soon as Sergeant Wade hung up, Nora checked her bedroom and the kitchen. The windows were all locked.

Then she ran to the living room. Just as she reached for the light switch, she saw the silhouette of a man backing away from the window. Nora left the room in darkness, moving slowly toward the bay window that faced the street. Through the rain and darkness it was hard for her to see the prowler clearly. He crossed the front yard, made a wide arc to avoid the street light, then walked to the other side of the road. Nora eased herself into the window seat, pulling her knees up to her chin. She was shivering.

The man crossed to the Craven house and stopped a few feet away from the front steps. He was staring at a darkened window on the second floor. The only light came from a window at the corner of the house by the garage. After several minutes he mounted the front steps. Then a smaller figure, who Nora guessed was Martin, opened the door. In the faint glow of light coming from the Cravens' kitchen, Nora could just make out the face of the man as he turned to close the door. It was Cecil McNab, that creepy old man from the dump, Nora thought. But what was he doing way over here? And why was he spying on her? Nora did not call Mr. Craven. She sat by the window and waited.

*

On the way home from the hospital, Dr. Lane was trying to console his wife. The tests had shown nothing. Antihistamines had not helped Tony's extreme sensitivity to light and heat. And the boy was behaving strangely, pacing his cold dark room like a caged animal. Mrs. Lane wanted to bring Tony home, but her husband insisted he stay where he was for observation. Besides, he had told her, if the condition turned out to be contagious, he did not want Nora exposed. The car turned onto Willoughby Street.

"There's a police car in front of the house!" Mrs. Lane said with alarm. The car had barely come to a halt when she bolted from her seat, running up the driveway.

Inside, a policeman was sitting in the kitchen with Nora. Nora ran to her mother, putting her arms around her waist.

"What's wrong?" Nora's mother looked from one to the other. The policeman stood up and closed his pad.

"The young lady reported seeing a prowler."

"Are you all right?" Mrs. Lane brushed the bangs back from Nora's forehead. Nora nodded. Dr. Lane walked in behind them, followed by a second policeman.

"Ed, can I see you a minute?" The first policeman joined the other in the hall. They talked in low voices. Dr. Lane sat down by the kitchen table and took Nora by the hand.

"Nora, Officer Pratt just came back from talking to Mr. Craven."

"Mr. Craven?" Nora's mother interrupted anxiously. Dr. Lane continued to look at Nora, speaking gently.

"Are you sure it wasn't someone else?"

Nora looked uncertainly from her father to her mother. "Dad, I know it was Cecil. Marty let him into the house. Didn't they ask him?"

"Martin was asleep, Nora. And Mr. Craven showed the policeman around the house. Cecil wasn't there."

"But I *saw* him. I saw Marty let him in. Ask him."

"He was asleep, Nora. And no one else was in the house but Martin and his father. Mr. Craven did say he heard something in his yard a while ago and went out to look around. Maybe he heard the prowler too, and just possibly, because of the dark and the storm, you mistook Mr. Craven for Cecil when he went back into the house."

Nora frowned with frustration. "You don't believe me."

"Of course we believe you. It's just that it's very dark out. It would be easy to make a mistake like that. The prowler could have been one of the neighborhood kids getting a jump on Halloween."

Nora pulled her hand away from her father. "I *know* what I saw," she said stubbornly, walking from the room. A moment later they heard her door close at the end of the hall.

"We'll be going now, Dr. Lane." Officer Pratt stood in the doorway. Nora's father showed the men out.

"We'll drive around the neighborhood. If we turn up anything else, we'll let you know."

Mrs. Lane followed them out to the hall.

"By the way" — Officer Pratt paused at the door — "I wonder if you'd mind taking a look at my boy. He seems to have come down with something. He's got some funny looking rash, and just sleeps all day."

"I'll stop by tomorrow on my way to the hospital," Dr. Lane replied. When the door closed, Mrs. Lane took her husband's hand.

"Mark, why would she think Hartford Craven was Cecil?"

"Can you think of a better candidate for the bogeyman?

Being alone in the house, in this storm, with some smart-alecky kid peering through the window . . . it doesn't take much to get the imagination going."

"But she seemed so sure."

"Don't you think Hartford would know if Cecil had been in the house? Janet, it's pitch black out there." Dr. Lane shrugged. "She had to be mistaken."

*

Standing at her window Nora stared angrily out at the rain. The footprints she had seen earlier had been washed away, leaving only the trail of prints from the policeman who searched the yard. As she watched, even these filled with rain and began to disappear before her eyes. Let them believe what they want, Nora thought defiantly. She knew it had been Cecil, but why had he been spying on her, she wondered with a chill. And what was he doing with Martin? Whatever they were up to, Nora decided, they were being careful to hide it.

10

An Ally

MONDAY MORNING, Nora waited anxiously on the bench for Maxine. Audrey Quinn sat nearby at the bottom of the stairs. Several other girls were with her. They were whispering. Nora nervously opened a book and pretended to read.

"I bet she made it up. Just a prank to get some attention."

"I don't think so. Dad said she really sounded scared."

Nora glanced over her shoulder. It was Karen Wade who was speaking. Audrey's group generally didn't associate with the younger girls, but everyone listened attentively to Sergeant Wade's daughter.

"And he said somebody else reported a prowler last night."

"But who'd want to spy on Nora Lane?" another girl commented.

"Really," someone else said a bit too loudly, "what a waste of time."

"Shh," Audrey warned, glancing over at Nora.

When the bell rang, Maxine was still nowhere in sight. Reluctantly, Nora picked up her books and started inside. As she passed Audrey and her friends, a few of them giggled. Nora walked quickly ahead.

The morning seemed to drag on forever. When the recess bell rang, Nora waited for the room to empty, then took off her glasses and rested her head on her desk. What did she care, she thought to herself, she never liked any of them anyway.

A familiar voice called through the door, "What are you doing in here? It's recess!" Nora rubbed the tears from her eyes and looked up. Maxine was walking toward her.

"Where were you?" Nora's eyes seized on her friend and followed her into the room.

"I was at the dentist's. My mother didn't tell me about it till this morning so I wouldn't lose any sleep over it. I just got out. See, no cavities!" Maxine curled her lip up in a toothy smile. Nora was sullen.

"Hey, what's the matter?" Maxine sat in the seat across the aisle. Nora put her glasses back on and squinted across at her. After a few moments of deliberation, she stammered, "You won't believe me either. I know you won't."

"What? The story about the cat?"

Nora shook her head.

"Then what? Tell me," Maxine coaxed her. Knowing

how quickly gossip traveled, Nora decided she'd better tell Max about Cecil before she heard it from someone else.

"Well?" By the time she finished, her voice was trembling. "What do you think?" she asked timidly.

Max looked thoughtful, then said, "Do you want me to be honest?"

Nora's heart sank. "I knew you wouldn't believe me."

"I didn't say that. But you have to admit, it's all a little hard to swallow. Two nights ago the Cravens' cat disappears in a puff of smoke, then last night that crazy old man from the dump goes prowling around in the pouring rain and peeking into your windows. Then he walks big as life right into the Cravens' house, only nobody can find him. And Marty, who supposedly let him in, doesn't know anything about it."

"No one asked him," Nora corrected. "They said he was asleep. Or more likely, pretending to sleep."

"You're positive it wasn't like your father said, mistaking Marty's father for Cecil?"

Nora nodded. "Well, do you believe me or not?" Nora's eyes were pleading.

Maxine sighed. "What can I say? I have to; otherwise, I don't see why you'd be acting like this."

Nora exhaled with relief.

"But," Maxine added, "I'd like to know why Marty would let Cecil into the house. None of it makes any sense. I think we should pay Marty a visit."

"We can't. My parents would never allow it. Dad said

whatever Marty and Tony have might be contagious."

"Then we'll have to do some prowling of our own." The bell rang and Maxine stood up to go back to her seat. "Tonight. As soon as it gets dark enough. We'll talk more on the way home."

*

"If I have to figure out one more hypotenuse I'll turn into a triangle." Maxine slammed her math book shut and sprawled at the foot of Nora's bed.

"Huh?" Nora's glasses had slid to the tip of her nose, giving her a split image of Maxine.

"Never mind. How's the English going?"

"I'm still stuck on the first poem. Max, I just can't concentrate. I keep thinking about spying on the Cravens."

"Here, let me see it."

Nora leaned across the bed and handed the book to Maxine.

"It's almost time to go. You'll never get that math done, Nora. Here, you better copy mine." She passed her homework sheet over to Nora. "Let's see now. 'Fall, leaves, fall; die, flowers, away; Lengthen night and shorten day.' This Brontë lady's a regular barrel of laughs." Maxine read the rest of the poem through to herself silently. "Hmm. I'm not sure I get it, either. Maybe we can figure it out by the last two lines."

Nora squinted over her glasses. "You can only do that with sonnets, when there's a poetic couplet at the end, remember?"

"Did you already try it?" Maxine asked.

"No, but it's not a sonnet."

"Then copy, and let me worry about this." After a few more minutes, Maxine broke the silence. "She loves the fall, and the night, and she especially likes the bad weather."

"How'd you get that?" Nora looked up again.

"The last two lines, like I told you. Listen: 'I shall sing when night's decay/Ushers in a drearier day.'"

"Typical of Schumann" — Nora frowned — "to make us read something like that."

When the sky darkened, Nora called up to her mother. "Max has to go home! I'm going to walk part way with her!"

"Don't take too long!" her mother called back down.

Nora stepped outside first, buttoning her coat to the collar. Maxine followed. The light from the street lamp glowed weakly through the creeping fog. In case anyone might be watching them from the Craven house, the two girls started down Willoughby Street.

Nora paid close attention to the sidewalk, carefully avoiding the worms that had surfaced after last night's rain, but Maxine kept watch on the Craven house. When they came to the end of the block, they crossed the street, then backtracked through the woods and slipped through the gate to the Cravens' driveway. Together, they crept along the side of the garage to the back yard.

"See anything yet?" Nora asked, plunging her hands into the warmth of her coat pockets.

"No," Maxine whispered back. "We have to get closer

to the house. I just hope we don't run into Cecil out here."

Nora shivered. Like a shadow, she followed Max along the back wall of the garage. Leaves crunched beneath their feet.

"I'm getting cold, Max."

"Shh." Maxine looked up at the gloomy old house. Gray shingles had broken off and lay scattered across the yard. It was badly in need of repair.

"Max, I'm not so sure this was a good idea. What if we get caught?"

"We will," Maxine whispered, "if you don't stop talking."

"But all the curtains are drawn. How are we going to see anything?"

Maxine hushed her, then darted across the gap between the garage and the side of the house. A rustling sound came from the roof above. Startled, Nora froze and looked up. A cluster of pigeons were fighting for space beneath the eaves. Nora looked about for Max, then jumped at the sudden shrill chatter of a squirrel scurrying along the gutter.

Maxine's footsteps faded in soft crunching sounds as she made her way through the leaves. Nora pulled her coat tighter against the chill. Full night had come.

"Max?" Nora squinted through the darkness. "Max, where are you?" she called softly. The fog and the dark made it impossible now to see more than a few feet away. With her hand before her, Nora felt her way along a hedge that grew at the back of the house. After several yards, she spotted a dim shaft of light pouring through a window by the back door. She pushed through the hedge and flattened herself to the side of the house. Slowly, she edged her way along. Just before the light, she came to a bulkhead. She could vaguely see the stairs on the other side.

"Darn it, Max, where are you?" Then she felt someone's breath on the back of her neck. Before she could turn, a hand clamped over her mouth.

"Shh," Maxine hissed. When she let go, Nora exhaled deeply.

"Why did you do that?" she whispered angrily. Maxine gestured toward the window by the back stairs, then moved out of the hedges and waved her friend to follow. She crept around the bulkhead and started up the stairs. The wood was old and rotting, giving a little under Maxine's weight. When she reached the top, she motioned for Nora to join her.

"We can't both fit. You look first," Nora whispered from the stoop. With one hand pressed against the door, Maxine grasped the window sill with the other. She leaned out just far enough to peer through a corner of the window.

Hartford Craven was sitting by himself at the kitchen table. His head was slumped forward, supported by one arm. Dirty dishes were stacked in the sink, and pans lined the counter. The table was strewn with cups and spoons and several empty cracker boxes. Mr. Craven looked much thinner than Maxine remembered. Suddenly, his face turned toward the window. She ducked her head below the sill.

"What is it?" Nora whispered.

"I think he might have seen me. We better get out of here."

A chair scraped across the floor, followed by approaching footsteps. At that moment, the sound of creaking hinges came from the bulkhead. Maxine lost her balance and jumped to the hedges below. A silhouette appeared in the window. Mr. Craven was peering out at them.

Maxine scrambled to her feet and dragged Nora across the lawn. Neither of them looked back till they were hidden behind a wide oak that grew at the edge of the yard.

The back door swung open. Mr. Craven stepped outside and looked across the lawn. After a moment he went back in and closed the door behind him.

"That was close." Maxine sighed. "For a minute I thought we were going to get caught."

"We almost did," Nora whispered nervously, "by whoever was coming out of the cellar."

"The cellar? What are you talking about?"

"Didn't you hear the cellar door opening?"

"Do you mean that creaking sound? I thought it was just a tree." All around them branches moaned and swayed against the wind.

"It was the door to the bulkhead," Nora whispered. "I saw it move."

"Come on. Let's get out of here."

Nora clutched her friend's arm as they stumbled through the underbrush.

"Max, I think someone is following us," she whispered nervously when they reached the street.

Maxine glanced over her shoulder back into the brush. "There's nothing there." She shuddered. "Anyway, we saw Mr. Craven go back inside. Darn it. I hope he couldn't tell it was me. I feel like such a jerk."

"But Max, it was your idea." Nora was beginning to shiver.

"I know, don't remind me." The icy wind rushed all around them, tossing up leaves and stinging their eyes. Maxine shoved her hands in her pockets and shuddered. A branch snapped behind them.

"What was that?" Nora jerked her head around.

"I wish you'd stop it. You're making me jumpy," Maxine scolded, but she looked back again anyway. "I better start home or my mother will shoot me."

Nora walked briskly to keep up with her.

"Where are you going?" Maxine pulled up short.

"With you. I'm not walking home alone!"

"But you only live across the street!" Maxine sighed. Then both girls' ears pricked to the sound of crunching leaves.

"Max, I don't think either of us should walk alone."

"I'm not going to walk. I'm going to run." Maxine started to turn just as the headlights of a car flashed around the corner. Both girls were caught in the glare. The car slowed and pulled up to the curb. It was Nora's father's car. He leaned across and rolled down the window.

"Why are you two standing out here?"

"My bodyguard was going to walk me part way home," Maxine replied wryly.

"It's freezing. Why don't you both hop in and I'll drive you home." Without hesitation, Maxine and Nora piled into the front seat. Dr. Lane swung the car around and drove back down Willoughby Street. As they turned the corner, Maxine looked back. Nora felt her stiffen. Maxine nudged her and gestured over her shoulder. Nora glanced back just in time to see Cecil stepping out of the bushes a few feet from where they'd been talking.

"Nora, are you all right? You're shaking," Dr. Lane asked. Nora faced forward in her seat.

"I think I'm catching a cold," she answered, gripping the hand of her friend. Maxine squeezed back securely.

*

Dinner at the Lane house that evening was tense. Nora's parents discussed several new cases of children with symptoms identical to Tony's. One of these had been Officer Pratt's son. Another was Peter Wade.

Nora's throat felt sore when she swallowed. While her parents talked on she wondered if she wasn't coming down with a cold.

"There may be others," her father went on, "but in this season people might shrug it off as the flu or an allergy."

"Mom, I don't feel well," Nora interrupted, coughing into her hand. Mrs. Lane pressed her palm to Nora's forehead.

"Mark, she does feel a little warm." She looked at her husband uneasily. After taking Nora's temperature, Dr.

Lane gave her some cough medicine and her mother helped her to bed.

Later, when her mother checked back in on her, Nora was sleeping soundly. Mrs. Lane crossed the room and opened the window a bit for air. Despite her husband's reassurances, she could not help worrying that Nora might be coming down with the same thing that Tony had.

*

In the middle of the night, Nora woke feeling very cold. Sitting up she saw that the window over her desk was wide open. Groggy with sleep, she pulled a blanket over her shoulders and started from bed to close it. Halfway across the room she heard something stirring behind her. She turned her head slowly. A figure was crouched in the corner. Nora backed up to her desk. When the figure exhaled, its breath poured out in a glowing stream. It began to straighten up, moving toward her. Nora's hand darted to the lamp on her desk and flicked it on. It was Martin.

His tongue flickered over his lips like a snake's and his eyes darted wildly, unseeing. His pale skin turned blotchy, then blistered as if it was being burned. Nora stepped backward into a corner, too frightened to make a sound.

With one arm Martin shielded his eyes, the pupils grotesquely enlarged. With the other he flailed the air as if he were blind, groping for the window. Finding it, he sprang through the hedges and darted across the lawn. Nora ran to the window, quickly pushed it closed, and latched it.

Hurrying to the stairs to wake her parents, she abruptly stopped. Through the window by the door, she could see Martin entering the house across the street. The clock in the hall read 4:00 A.M. She wanted to shout, but with instant and utter frustration, she knew it would do no good. By the time she roused her parents, Martin would be back in his bed. They hadn't believed about Cecil; it wasn't likely they'd believe her now. Never had she felt more alone.

11

Something Called Soul

THE NEXT MORNING, Mrs. Lane woke Nora with a breakfast tray.

"You're up early." She placed the tray on Nora's night table. "Nora?" She gently shook her by the shoulder. Nora woke with a start, drawing herself back against the headboard.

"I'm sorry I startled you." Mrs. Lane put the back of her hand to Nora's forehead. She was running a slight fever, and her face felt damp and warm. "When I saw your light I thought you were awake."

Nora pulled the blankets up around her.

"Are you all right?" Her mother watched her with concern. Nora nodded, wishing Maxine was there, then reached for the cup of hot chocolate on her tray. She inhaled the steam rising from the cup. When she drank, the hot liquid soothed the soreness in her throat. She cradled the cup on her chest and closed her eyes, feeling the warmth penetrate her hands.

Later that afternoon, Maxine called. Mrs. Lane carried the hall extension into Nora's room and left it on her bed.

"What happened to you?" Maxine asked. "I've been worried sick all day."

"I've got a cold."

"That's what your mother said. Seems like a lot of kids were out sick today."

"I'm surprised she didn't think I was just imagining it," Nora remarked sarcastically, sniffing back her runny nose.

"It sounds pretty real to me. When are you coming back to school?"

"Dunno." Nora blew her nose.

"Nora, I couldn't sleep last night. I kept thinking about seeing Cecil and everything you told me."

"Max, I'm scared." Nora started to cry, blurting out the story of Martin's visit.

"Geez, Nora! Why didn't you tell me right away? Do you want me to come over?"

"My mother probably wouldn't want you to, not while I have this cold. Max, what are we going to do?" Nora sobbed.

"Nora, this is serious. Maybe I should try talking to my parents."

"I doubt it would do much good. What could we prove?" Nora sniffed.

"I suppose you're right. But I still wish there was someone we could talk to. We can't just go on like nothing's wrong."

"There *is* someone," Nora said anxiously. "I've been thinking about Mrs. Cribbins. She must know something. Otherwise, why would she have left them?"

"Of course!" Maxine said excitedly. "No one's been able to figure out why she left. And wasn't it the same day that Marty first got sick?"

"Yes. And whatever's going on, this sickness is a part of it. If only you saw what happened to Marty when I turned on the light. It's like it isn't him anymore. And . . . and now Tony . . ." Nora began to sob again, quietly. "Max, what's happening? What was he doing in my room?"

"I don't know. But I'm going to see Mrs. Cribbins right now."

"What are you going to say?"

"I don't know yet. But after what happened last night, we have to do something fast."

"Max, do you think it will happen again?"

"I don't know. But I think you should put your light on as soon as it gets dark. And leave it on. That's one thing on your side. You know that light can stop him."

"Max, be careful."

"I will. I'll call you as soon as I get back." Maxine hung up.

*

Maxine had met Mrs. Cribbins only once, a few years earlier at a church bake sale, and she'd done a lot of growing since then. As she put on her coat, she wondered if the elderly housekeeper would even remember her. Stepping outside, Maxine shivered at the cold dampness in the air. To keep warm, she jogged the eight blocks to Covendale center.

A bell at the top of the glass door chimed as Maxine entered the hardware store. Mr. Sweeney glanced over his shoulder. "Now, what can I do for you?" he asked, smiling.

"I wanted to see Mrs. Cribbins." Maxine walked up to the counter. She was as tall as the little man behind it.

"Don't I know you?" Mr. Sweeney squinted behind his bifocals.

"I'm Maxine Boyko. I haven't been here for a while, Mr. Sweeney."

"Little Max!" Mr. Sweeney bellowed. "Of course! You used to come in here every summer to buy those Fourth of July sparklers."

Maxine blushed at the memory.

"Course, that must have been some time ago. You've sprung up like a beanpole."

Maxine grew redder. She knew Mr. Sweeney wasn't making fun of her, but she was self-conscious about her height.

"Now, what was it you wanted?"

"I came to see Mrs. Cribbins."

"Ah, Mrs. Cribbins. Well, she should be glad to see you. Hasn't had a visitor since she moved in." Mr. Sweeney walked around the counter. "There are stairs outside at the back, but today you go right in through there. You'll find another staircase." He pointed at the curtains. "Mind you don't trip over the boxes, though."

"Thanks, Mr. Sweeney."

He looked after her, rubbing his chin. When the curtains closed behind her, he grinned.

"Little Max. Who'd of guessed it? Why, that girl used to stand tiptoe and still not see over the counter."

At the top of the cluttered stairway, a bare bulb hung before a narrow door speckled with mildew. Maxine knocked softly, still wondering what she would say to the old house-keeper. After a few moments, she knocked again, louder. The sound of shuffling came from the other side of the door, then scraping as the chain slid from the lock. The door swung open.

"What is it, Sa . . ." Mrs. Cribbins cut herself short, taking a step back. Maxine and the housekeeper stared at one another awkwardly.

"I'm Maxine Boyko, Mrs. Cribbins." Maxine knotted her fingers behind her.

"Boyko?" Mrs. Cribbins repeated the name as though it was a foreign word. Her eyes narrowed beneath silver brows.

"My mother is Alice Boyko."

With head cocked to one side, the small woman tugged at her lip and looked thoughtfully at Maxine.

"Alice, yes, I know Alice. Alice had a little girl."

Maxine flushed pink again.

"That was me, Mrs. Cribbins."

"You!" Mrs. Cribbins said with disbelief.

"Well" — Maxine slumped her shoulders, growing redder — "you saw me a couple of years ago. I sort of grew since then." She looked down at herself, wishing she were a foot shorter.

"Don't look a thing like her," the housekeeper said, matter-of-factly.

"But I grew up!" Maxine said defensively, standing up straighter.

"So you have." Mrs. Cribbins smiled at last, a glimmer of recognition in her eyes. "I'm sorry, come in. I wasn't expecting anyone. You took me by surprise."

"I should have called you first," Maxine apologized, "but it was urgent."

Mrs. Cribbins closed and latched the door. Maxine found herself in a tiny kitchen with a folding card table by the window and one chair.

"Here." Mrs. Cribbins pulled a foot stool over from beneath the sink. "Just moved in a week ago. Haven't much furniture. You'll have to sit on that." She went to the stove and turned off a pan of boiling water. "I can only offer you tea. Unless you'd like a glass of milk?"

"No, thank you. I can't stay long." Maxine sat down on the stool and tucked her legs beneath the table. Mrs. Cribbins dropped a teabag in a cup and filled it with water.

"Takes a while to get settled. Sam loaned me a bed and an old dresser. All I brought with me was a suitcase." The housekeeper sat down across from her. There was a Bible open on the table.

"Mrs. Cribbins, why did you leave the Cravens?" Maxine asked in a rush. Mrs. Cribbins stiffened. Maxine shifted her long legs, jerking the table and splashing a bit of hot tea over the lip of Mrs. Cribbins's cup. "How do you know the Cravens?" The housekeeper eyed Max suspiciously.

"I go to school with Marty."

"Martin." Mrs. Cribbins sighed, fingering the Bible.

"You left the day that Marty got sick. And whatever he has, now Tony Lane has it too."

"What?" The housekeeper's small round face paled. She looked startled. Maxine couldn't decide whether she resembled a ghost or an angel, with her white face surrounded by a halo of brittle silver curls. Her small hand, speckled with brown spots like a sparrow's egg, gripped the edge of the table. "The Lane boy is sick?"

"The light makes him break out in a rash and it hurts his eyes. He can't eat anything, either. Nora, that's Tony's sister, said they have to keep him in a dark cold room. He's in the hospital."

Mrs. Cribbins's eyes began to water. Her lips moved silently in prayer.

"Mrs. Cribbins, what's wrong with them? Nora's father told her it was just an allergy."

"An allergy!" The old woman half laughed. "No wonder the boy is no better. They can't treat his soul with medicine."

"His soul?" Maxine wasn't even sure what the word meant. She imagined it had something to do with feeling, picturing an organ made only of light, roughly in the shape of a heart.

Mrs. Cribbins stared down at the Bible as she spoke. "I haven't talked about this with anyone. I didn't think anyone would believe me. Hartford Craven didn't, and he's right there with the boy. If he wouldn't listen, who else could I talk to?" The housekeeper closed the Bible in her lap. There were tears in her eyes.

"Mrs. Cribbins, I'm listening," Maxine said softly. "It might help if you could tell me what you knew."

The housekeeper looked up at Maxine and shook her head. "How can I explain it to you?" She stared across the table at the girl for several moments, then added, "You're so young. It will probably only frighten you, and it won't make any sense."

"Mrs. Cribbins, I'm already frightened. There's more that I haven't told you." The housekeeper looked at the girl curiously. "Something weird is going on, and Nora may be in danger. I thought you might be able to help us. Please, Mrs. Cribbins, tell me what you know." Maxine sat straighter, trying to give the impression of age beyond her thirteen years.

"Your friend is in danger? What kind of danger?"

"Please, Mrs. Cribbins, first tell me what you know."

The housekeeper nodded. "It started after Martin came home from a day out with his father. They'd done several errands for me in town, and I think they drove out to the dump. Yes, it was a week ago Saturday." Slowly the housekeeper told her of Martin's cramps, and about the argument that erupted between her and Martin's father. "The boy had always been a bit saucy, but basically, he was a good boy. Anyway, it was the next day, after I discovered the rash, that I began to notice the other change. The boy suddenly seemed so hostile. I tried to keep out of his way. I thought it was because of the rash that he was being so cranky. If that was all it was I could have forgiven; I would have understood. But later, after we'd gone to sleep, I awoke suddenly." As the housekeeper described the attack, Maxine shifted uncomfortably in her seat. She shuddered to think that the same thing had almost happened to Nora.

"Have you ever thought of death, of what it might be like?" the old woman was asking. Maxine shook her head. Occasionally the thought came to her, but she always pushed it aside.

"I know." Mrs. Cribbins continued, "You're young. And why should the young think about death? But I've thought about it often, more now that Mr. Cribbins is gone. I'm old. It's a natural preoccupation. When Martin . . . I say 'Martin,' but at the same time I knew it was no longer him. When Martin came to my room that night, I felt closer to death than at any other moment in my life. This is what's so hard to describe. When the boy mingled his breath with mine, it was like drowning. I felt as though the night had suddenly caved in around me. And then, all at once, it was in me, too. It was as if I was becoming part of it. I began to see tiny lights, like stars 'way off in the distance all around me. There seemed to be more and more of them. Then I realized, I was still in my room, and the light was coming from all the objects around me. It even came from the air. Then I smelled the flowers in the vase by my bed. They were wilting. But for some reason I felt drawn to them. In an odd way, it was like hunger. But a hunger for things dying." Mrs. Cribbins stopped herself. "I'm upsetting you."

Maxine was looking down at her hands. Unconsciously she had dug her nails into her palms.

"It's all right, Mrs. Cribbins. Go on." She had to hear as much as the old woman could tell her.

"There's little more to tell. I was caught somewhere between being devoured by this . . . this hunger, and becoming it. Somehow I managed to stop breathing. By not breathing, some of the sensation came back into my body, which had been feeling frozen, or numb. I don't know why exactly, but some impulse made me reach for the lamp by my bed. For a moment, when the light came on, I felt terrified. But it wasn't exactly my own terror. I mean, it was in me, but it wasn't mine. Martin must have run from the room. Immediately I felt sick and couldn't quite see. My eyes burned, and I began to cough up whatever it was that Martin had breathed into me. It wasn't enough to make me like him, but I know that's what he was trying to do."

"Mrs. Cribbins, why would Cecil McNab be at the Cravens'? Nora and I saw him there last night. And two nights ago, Nora saw him visiting Martin."

The housekeeper wiped her eyes and looked up. She seemed confused. "Cecil? I don't know what you mean. He's never come to the house before. And Martin always made fun of the man."

"Mrs. Cribbins, you have to help us. Somehow Cecil is involved in this too. And Marty's trying to get at Nora. Last night he crawled in through her window, but she turned on her light and scared him away."

"Is she all right?" Mrs. Cribbins's voice was strained.

"She was pretty shaken, but the worst is that she can't talk to anyone. A few nights ago, Nora's mother accidentally ran over Nikki when they were driving Tony to the hospital. Nora stayed at home. She saw it happen. She said some sort of weird glowing smoke poured out of Nikki's body. Then the cat disappeared. But she's sure it was dead." The old woman stiffened, but Maxine quickly went on. "The night after that, when we had that big thunderstorm, Nora saw Cecil prowling around her house. That was when she saw Marty letting him in. She told her parents, but they just thought it was Marty's father she saw. Mr. Craven acts as though he doesn't know what's going on, and for a while I couldn't completely believe it, either. Then Nora and I did some spying on the Cravens. When we left the yard, we saw Cecil following us. And now, after last night, we know we have to do something. Nora could be in danger. Please, Mrs. Cribbins, you have to help us."

Tears reappeared in the old woman's eyes. "There's nothing I can do but pray."

"Then you have to tell someone who can help. They'd believe you."

"The people in this town think I'm a senile old woman," Mrs. Cribbins said sadly. "I hear them whispering behind my back. If it weren't for the kindness of Mr. Sweeney, I'd probably be out on the street. And even if they did believe me, I doubt it would do much good. If you'd been through what I have, you'd understand. It's not just a sickness. It changes people."

"But we have to do something!" Maxine was getting excited. "If we don't, this thing could spread through the whole town!" A knock sounded at the door.

"It must be Sam. I'm sorry, Maxine. We'll have to finish this conversation another time." Mrs. Cribbins got up to unlatch the door. Mr. Sweeney walked into the kitchen, grinning from ear to ear. He was holding a paper funnel, faded blue with gold stars stamped across it. Several thin gray rods jutted out from the top.

"You'll never guess what I dug up," he announced, beaming, "sparklers!"

Maxine tried to smile, hoping he wouldn't see how upset she was.

"Don't even know if they still work. Why don't you light one?" He fished in his pocket for a book of matches and handed them to her. Not wanting to hurt his feelings, Maxine walked out the back door with him. The moment she lit one, it began throwing out tiny star bursts that hissed as it burned its way down the stem. She tossed it over the railing, casting a shower of blue and golden sparks into the night.

"Thank you, Mr. Sweeney, I forgot how beautiful they were."

"Don't go burning them all up at once like you used to." He grinned, holding them out to her like a bouquet of flowers.

"Thank you. I better go home now. It's getting dark."

"Good seeing you. Brings back memories, it does." Mr. Sweeney smiled.

"Be careful," Mrs. Cribbins called from behind him.

12

Whistling in the Dark

MAXINE WALKED SLOWLY homeward, pulling her jacket tight against the cold as she thought over her conversation with Mrs. Cribbins. For a moment, when the sparkler had blazed its blue-gold light, her fears seemed to vanish, like a bad dream chased away by the morning. But as darkness crept in around her, the nightmare seemed more real than ever. And Mrs. Cribbins had said it was hopeless. How could she tell this to Nora, she wondered. Could there really be no hope?

Maxine looked up at the first star of the night. She had always seen night as a glittering mystery, filled with magic and hope and dreams. Now it was suddenly frightening. A night of hunger, she thought, recalling the housekeeper's words. A hunger for things dying.

As Maxine walked to the end of Center Street, the street lights came on. She had stayed with Mrs. Cribbins longer than she'd planned. She had hoped to be home before dark. The Baptist church stood by itself at the end of the block, a dim glow pouring from its high arched windows. I can only pray, the housekeeper had said. Maxine had never thought much about praying. Of course, she sang with the congregation on Sundays. But to Maxine, church was as much a place for bake sales and bingo, as it was a place for prayer. At the corner, she stopped. The organ master was practicing a psalm. Maxine had sung it many times before, but she had never really listened to the words. Now she sang them to herself, noting for the first time the song's meaning,

> "We praise the sacred light of life,
> Amidst the darkness, burning bright.
> We bare this shield with all its might,
> Against the armies of the night.
> Glorious light, giver of life,
> *Dona nobis pacem.*"

As she walked on, she continued to sing to herself. When she was five blocks from home, turning the corner onto Caldecot Street, she heard the sound of glass breaking and the street light went out.

A short figure stepped out from a cluster of bushes a few yards away and started walking toward her. Maxine sighed with relief at the familiar face. It was Ray Gillette, one of the boys from school. But then she noticed that he was in his pajamas. Maxine picked up her pace apprehensively. As she tried to pass him, the boy blocked her path. Someone sprang at her from behind, dragging her into the bushes. Her legs buckled under and she fell.

Rough hands turned her over, pinning her shoulders to the ground. Two faces crowded over her. Above them, the dim beacon from a lighthouse two miles away swept across the sky. Suddenly, lips were pressed to her mouth, blocking the passage of air. While the two boys crouched about her shoulders, Maxine struggled to pull the cone of sparklers from her coat pocket. Her head throbbed. A cold wetness seeped over her mouth. Teeth scraped against her lips, trying to force them open. Her hands blindly fought with the matches. She struck one, immediately setting the whole book ablaze.

The two boys backed away, their hands covering their eyes. Using the flaming matchbook, Maxine quickly lit the cone of sparklers which erupted in a torch of hissing sparks. She waved it in the air, driving the boys farther away. Then she stood and ran, not stopping until she was home again. She pushed through the door, sinking against it as it closed behind her. It wasn't till then that Maxine felt the pain in her fingers. Holding up her hand, she saw that the matches had burned them.

*

"Max again," Mrs. Lane announced, opening Nora's door. She set the hall phone down on the night table, then crossed the room to close the curtains. Nora lifted the phone to her ear but said nothing. She was waiting for her mother to leave, but Mrs. Lane began to sort through the dirty clothes on the floor of her closet.

"Mom" — Nora covered the mouthpiece of the phone with her hand — "please, not while I'm on the phone," she pleaded. Her mother smiled and nodded, then left and shut the door.

"Did you see her?" Nora asked anxiously into the phone.

"Yes, but . . ." Maxine paused, then continued nervously, "Nora, two kids from school attacked me on the way home." Her voice quavered as she rapidly told the story. "The only thing that saved me was those sparklers. Nora, it was as though they knew just where to catch me."

"Are you all right?"

"I'm still shaking. And my fingers are burned. But I've got on every light in the house. I'm O.K. I just wish my parents were home."

"Are you going to tell them?"

"As soon as they get home."

Nora relaxed with relief. At last, maybe they'd be getting somewhere.

"What happened with Mrs. Cribbins?"

"She won't be any help. She clutched her Bible the whole time we talked and said all she could do was pray. A lot of good that will do. I was singing a hymn when they got me."

"Doesn't she know what's happening?"

"Oh, she knows, all right. Marty attacked her, too. That's why she left the Cravens." As well as she could, Maxine retold Mrs. Cribbins's story.

"Then why won't she help us?"

"She's afraid everyone will just think she's got a screw loose. She does have that reputation."

"But if the three of us tell the same story, someone will have to believe us," Nora said anxiously.

"I know. I'll try to talk to her again." Maxine paused. "Nora, I just heard the front door close. My father must be home."

"Good luck."

"Don't worry. Dad's going to be livid when he hears what they pulled on me. I better go. Remember, keep a light on in your room tonight. It's your only protection."

"Let me know what happens."

"If I don't call back, I'll come by after school tomorrow."

After hanging up, Nora put on her robe and slippers and started toward the bathroom. Halfway down the hall, she stopped. Her parents were talking in the kitchen.

"Eight more cases today. I swear it's becoming an epidemic."

"But what's causing it?" Her mother's voice was strained.

"I don't know, Janet. There are three of us working on it now. I hope that will speed things up. We've ruled out allergies. All those tests came back negative. Could be a new strain of virus, or possibly a toxin in the environment. Something they all might easily have gotten into. In the meantime, I've started Tony and the others on massive doses of antibiotics. It'll be several days though before I know if they're effective."

"Have any adults come down with it yet?"

"None that we know of. So far it's just hitting the kids. There's a common link here somewhere. We've already checked the water supply at school for microorganisms and metallic levels. And we've checked out the cafeteria for bacteria. Someone's going down tomorrow to take soil samples from the playground. We're following up on everything we can think of. I can't help feeling somehow that the answer is right under my nose."

The phone rang. Nora started down the hall to get it, but her mother had already picked up the kitchen extension.

"It's for you, Mark."

"Hello, Dr. Lane speaking." After a brief silence, he said, "I'll be right over. In the meantime, all you can do is see that she's comfortable. Keep the room dark and keep her cool." Then he hung up.

"Who was that?"

"Karen, Sergeant Wade's daughter, has it. I told him I'd be right over." Nora slipped into the bathroom as her father walked out to the hall.

"Mark" — Nora's mother walked out after him — "can't we bring Tony home? I don't see what good it does, keeping him in the hospital."

"I explained it before. If this thing is contagious, we have to keep him isolated."

"But I can do as much as a nurse," Nora's mother pleaded. "I'd keep Nora away from him."

"That's what Mrs. Wade said when Peter became ill. Now his sister has it. I don't want Nora exposed."

"I know." Mrs. Lane sighed. "It's just that I miss him."

Dr. Lane embraced her, "We'll lick it. There's got to be an answer to all this. We'll just have to be patient."

Mrs. Lane walked her husband to the door. There is an answer, Nora thought to herself, and it had something to do with Cecil. Maybe now her father would listen. When he got back from the Wades', Nora decided, she would have to make him listen.

Nora ate alone with her mother that night, barely picking at her meal. After watching Nora push her food around her plate, her mother sent her back to bed. Nora tried to read, but couldn't. Instead, she watched the clock. She wondered if her father was safe, anxious for him to return. At ten-thirty, her mother turned out the downstairs lights, then came to tuck her in.

"Isn't Dad back yet?" Nora asked.

Her mother shook her head. "Nora, it's late. You ought to be asleep." She put her hand to Nora's head to check for fever.

"I can't sleep. After being in bed all day, I'm just not tired, Mom."

"Don't you think it would help if you put out the light?"

"I thought I'd read till Dad got home." Nora reached for a book on her night table. Her mother intercepted it.

"How do you expect to get over that cold if you keep yourself up all night reading? Lights out."

"Aw, Mom, please?"

"No argument, young lady. I mean it. I don't want you getting any sicker." Her mother pulled the cord on the lamp. Then she bent to kiss Nora's forehead. "I'm sorry, baby. I don't mean to be so cranky. It's just I'm worried about you and your brother, and my nerves are all on edge. Try to sleep, O.K.?"

"Mom, at least will you leave my door open a crack?"

Mrs. Lane sat down on the edge of the bed.

"Still having nightmares?"

"Sort of. It might help if I had the light on."

Her mother reached into the pocket of her apron.

"I'll make a deal with you. I'll let you have this if you promise to leave the light off and try to get some sleep." She held out a small chain with something that looked like a lipstick tube dangling at the end.

"What is it?"

"It's my keychain flashlight." Her mother pressed one end. It projected a small shaft of light onto Nora's pillow.

Nora took the small cylinder and pressed the button.

"Here." Mrs. Lane unsnapped the chain, then refastened it on Nora's wrist. Her mother's bright clear eyes shone warmly through the darkness. Nora wondered if she should just tell her mother now, rather than wait for her father to return.

"If only I had your imagination, maybe I'd be able to write something worthwhile," Mrs. Lane said teasingly, tucking the blankets up around her. No, Nora decided, it was better to wait. And once Max's father was on their side, her parents would have to believe. Her mother stood and left the room, leaving the door ajar.

*

As soon as Maxine told her father about the attack, he called the boys' parents. When he hung up, he turned and regarded her oddly.

"Are you sure it was Ray and Peter?" he asked.

"Why?" Maxine immediately sensed something was wrong.

"Because their parents said both boys have been sick in bed all day." Her father looked at her curiously. "Max," he asked, waiting for her to reply, "are you sure you saw their faces?"

"I told you, Dad. It was Ray and Peter. Both of them *live* right around the corner from where they got me."

"Max," he interrupted, "think. Could it have been anyone who looked like them?" How could she prove it? For the first time, Maxine could fully appreciate Nora's frustration. She looked at her father's worried face, searching for some way to convince him.

"I told you who it was!" She finally shrugged, realizing there was nothing more she could say.

Maxine did not call Nora, knowing this news would only upset her. As soon as supper was over, she went to her room to think. She had no doubt that it had been Ray and Peter. They must have *snuck* out, she realized, while their parents thought they were sleeping, and then slipped back home again while she was getting away. There was a lamp on her desk beneath the window. After her parents went up to bed, she removed the lamp shade, letting the bare bulb blaze like a beacon.

13

Tony Comes Home

NORA DOZED, in spite of the darkness, tossing restlessly and plagued by cruel dreams. She had no idea what time it was when she awoke, but there was a scratching sound coming from somewhere in the room. Nora leaned up on one elbow. After listening a moment, she realized it wasn't coming from inside the room, but from the window. She tried to ignore it, telling herself it was only a branch, and burrowed under the covers. But when the sound persisted she slipped from her bed and crossed quietly to the window. The scratching stopped. Defiantly, she held up the keychain light and yanked apart the curtains. She released her grip on the small tube dangling from her wrist. Tony's face was pressed to the glass.

"Nora, let me in." His hushed voice drifted like a chilly wind through the glass pane. It was barely recognizable;

dull and emotionless. "Why did you lock me out? Please, Nora. It's cold. Let me in." The boy's face had a strange look of urgency. Nora felt transfixed. The room around her seemed to be melting away. As if of its own volition, her hand moved toward the window lock. The latch turned, the window rose. The cold night air crept over the sill and wrapped itself around her.

Tony's hand caressed her face. His fingers slid to the back of her neck like icy rain, then tightened.

"Don't," Nora begged, her mind struggling but her body numb. "Please, Tony. Don't."

For a moment her brother faltered, loosening his grip. He frowned and cocked his head to the side, as if listening to other voices. His dark eyes seemed to clear a bit and his expression grew familiar. Then suddenly his gaze went blank and he grasped her. Nora felt his icy lips and blackness swam up all around her, scattering her memory like ashes in the wind. She slumped against the window sill.

Vaguely familiar faces hovered in the darkness above her. A crowd of hands, like fat pale spiders, were pulling her through the window.

"Nora?" A man's deep voice called from far away. A burning light jolted her like lightning. Warmth slowly poured back into her body as she fell.

"Nora!" Dr. Lane rushed toward her. The lamp by her bed was on. "What's the matter?" He kneeled beside her. Nora was coughing violently.

Her father pulled her close and briskly rubbed her back. A luminous dust speckled her father's coat where she coughed against his shoulder. Neither of them noticed the odd dust before it faded then disintegrated in the soft light from the lamp. When her breathing returned to normal, Nora's father pulled her up and rested her back against the wall. As it rippled in the wind, the hem of the curtain brushed her cheek.

"Baby? Are you all right?"

"Tony," Nora said weakly.

"What?" Her father slipped his arm around her and helped her back to bed.

"He's outside." Nora grasped her father's arm as he tucked her under the covers. "He made me open the window!" she said urgently. "They were trying to get me."

Dr. Lane looked at her curiously, then walked back to the window and looked out. The yard was empty. He closed and locked the window, then drew the curtains.

"Nora, you must have been dreaming. I heard you talking in your sleep on my way to the kitchen."

"I wasn't." Nora's lip trembled. "It was Tony. I saw him!"

"Nora," her father said soothingly, "you know your brother's in the hospital. It was only a dream. There's nothing out there." Dr. Lane pressed the back of his hand to Nora's forehead. "You don't have a fever. But that cough is sounding worse. Did you take your medicine?"

"The light! The light scared him away!" Nora continued, ignoring her father's question. Dr. Lane sat down at the side of her bed.

"How long have you been having these nightmares?"

"I'm not having nightmares!" Nora cried. Her father began to brush the hair away from her forehead, his brow creasing with worry.

"That's not what your mother tells me."

It was useless, Nora thought. Alone, she could never convince them. She could only protect herself and hope that Maxine, in the meantime, was having better luck.

"All right, I'm having nightmares," she said curtly.

"What are they about?"

"I can't remember. But I'm afraid of the dark," she said simply.

"But you've never been afraid of the dark. Not even when you were small. Nora, your mother and I are right upstairs. There's nothing to be afraid of." Her father stroked her cheek, then reached toward the lamp.

"No!" Nora begged. "Please don't turn off the light. I promise I'll be O.K. if you leave on the light." Her father withdrew his hand. For a long moment he just stared at her.

He relented. "All right, I'll leave it on for tonight." He kissed her and stood to leave. "But remember, Nora, dreams are only dreams. They can't hurt us. Now, try and go to sleep."

Nora turned her head away, feeling she might cry.

On his way to the stairs, Nora's father paused by the phone. He looked back at the light seeping out beneath Nora's door, then picked up the phone and dialed the hospital.

"This is Dr. Lane. Would you connect me with C ward, please."

After a moment, a woman's voice came on. "C ward, Nurse Halley speaking."

"Hello, Laura. It's Mark Lane. I wonder if you'd check in on Tony for me."

"Is something wrong?"

"No, I just want you to see if the boy's sleeping. Would you?"

"Hold on, I'll just be a minute." The nurse set the phone on the counter, then walked down the corridor to Tony's room. A strong breeze billowed the drapes around the open window. Laura crossed the darkened room, closed it all but a crack, then bent over the shape under the blankets on Tony's bed. "Tony?" she said softly. When there was no answer, she quietly left the room and returned to the nurses' station.

"Mark? He seems to be asleep."

"Thank you, Laura." Dr. Lane hung up and went to his room. Slowly he undressed in the dark and crawled in beside his wife. She stirred, then wakening, turned toward him.

"Mark? What time is it?"

"A little past midnight."

"Mark, I'm worried about Nora."

"I know. I am, too."

*

Throughout the town of Covendale, fourteen figures wandered separately through the night, many in nightclothes and barefooted, impervious to the damp and cold. At a glance one might have thought it was the moon that painted their faces so pale — the color of wheat in winter, dull and lifeless. These were the faces of hunger, spreading the night spore like a shadow over the earth.

An hour before dawn, Tony, like the others, began to feel the prickly heat of rash as the sky lightened to gray. He walked back through woods to the hospital, pushed open his window, and crawled back into his room. He took the pillows out from under his blanket, then climbed into bed to take refuge from the coming day.

*

After school the next day, Maxine walked directly to Nora's house. In the bright afternoon sun, the Craven house seemed less threatening. Walking by, Maxine stared bravely up the walk. She knew she was safe, for the moment. She imagined herself bursting in through the door, flying from room to room, drawing the drapes and opening all the windows. What that house needs, she thought to herself, is a good airing out.

"Hi, Max." Nora's mother was on her way out the door. Maxine cut across the lawn. "Nora's in the kitchen," Mrs. Lane told her, holding the door till the girl stepped inside.

"How's Tony?" Maxine looked at her through the screen.

"I don't know." Mrs. Lane sighed. "I was just on my way

to see him. I'm glad you came by. Nora could use some cheering up. She's been in the dumps all day."

Maxine found Nora sitting in her robe and slippers, staring at a plate of cold scrambled eggs.

"Why are you eating breakfast? Nora, it's after three." Maxine looked at her oddly.

"I just got up. How did it go?" Nora asked, suddenly perking up. When Maxine told her, Nora glanced down at her plate and sighed gloomily. "How's your hand?" she asked after a moment.

Maxine slipped into the chair next to her and examined the blisters on her fingers. "All right. How's your cold?"

"Better." Nora picked up her fork and scraped the eggs into a pile.

"Why don't you get dressed and we'll go for a walk?"

"I'm too tired." Nora mashed the eggs down, then spread them in a ring around the edge of her plate.

"I think those eggs have had it." Maxine grinned wryly. "Come on. The fresh air will wake you up."

"Oh, all right," Nora mumbled, pushing out her chair and shuffling down the hall. Maxine got up and followed her.

Nora slipped into her jeans and her sneakers, then pulled on a heavy woolen sweater. But outside, she only grew more sullen. She carefully avoided looking at the Craven house as she started across the lawn. Maxine followed her to the back yard, where she took a seat on the crumbling stone wall that bordered the brook. She frowned at the dark water, winding its way into the woods. Brightly colored leaves floated idly on the surface.

"Come on, Nora, what's the matter? You're not just tired. There's something you're not telling me."

"Tony came last night. He tried to make me one of them."

Maxine shivered. "Oh Nora." Her voice was full of sorrow. "We've got to stop this somehow. Whether anyone believes us or not!"

"They're too strong, Max. And there are too many of them." Nora still stared at the brook, feeling hope drift away like the leaves on its surface.

"Listen to me." Maxine took her friend's arm, pressing it till Nora looked at her. "We can stop it. There has to be a way. And we're the only ones who can do it."

"But what can we do? We're just two kids; we can't do anything alone. We'd need help. And who's going to help us if we can't get anyone to believe us?"

Maxine pressed harder. "There's no one else. We don't have a choice."

"Max, I'm just not strong enough. Tony's one of them, don't you see? I couldn't do anything to hurt him."

"But Nora, it isn't Tony. Whatever was Tony has been taken over by this thing. I told you what Mrs. Cribbins said. He's changed now."

"It's still Tony!" Nora said emphatically. "I felt it when I saw him. Max, I can't hurt him. Don't you understand?"

Maxine was silent. She looked thoughtful.

"See, it's hopeless," Nora said resolutely.

"No!" Maxine made Nora face her. "I've been thinking

this over all morning. There is something we can do. Up till now, everyone's been treating this thing exactly the way *it* wants to be treated. Since light causes those bad reactions, the parents of all these kids protect them from it, keeping them in dark rooms. But when Mrs. Cribbins was attacked, she said the light saved her. She said it hurt at first, but then it made her better."

"That's what happened to me when Dad turned on the light last night."

"Then you should see what I'm getting at." Maxine went on, "As far as we know, none of these kids has been exposed to light for more than a few minutes at most. They get away or someone turns the light out as soon as they start breaking out in that rash or complaining about their eyes. But no one knows what would happen if one of them was forced to *stay* in the light, for a longer time."

"But Max, if it's been growing in them for a while, maybe the light could really hurt them."

"So, what do you want? Take Mrs. Cribbins's suggestion and pray?" Maxine asked impatiently. "You know what good that does. Nora, we have to try this thing with the light. If you're right, if something of what these kids were still exists, a soul, or whatever you want to call it, then the light might cure them."

"And if I'm wrong?" Nora asked tensely.

"It's a risk we have to take. They still have to be stopped," Maxine answered flatly. "If they're not, everyone in Covendale could become infected. If *I* were one of them,

I'd want someone to take that risk. No matter what."

"I couldn't take the chance of hurting Tony," Nora persisted.

"We won't try it on Tony."

"Then who?"

"I know how this might sound. But it's the only way I could work myself up to the point where I could actually do it. Marty has tried to get at you once. He'll probably try again. Besides that, he's been infected the longest. It may even have started with him."

"But what if it backfires? What if it . . ."

"Marty, or whatever Marty has become, is dangerous," Maxine interrupted. "If he's attacked you and Mrs. Cribbins, he must have attacked others. Nora, you know he's probably responsible for Tony's becoming infected."

Nora stiffened. "I'm afraid, Max."

Maxine gripped her friend's hand and squeezed it. "So am I."

14

After the Sun Goes Down

LATER, WHEN MAXINE returned home, she tried to call Mrs.
Cribbins. But Mrs. Cribbins was paying a visit to the Baptist church. After praying silently in a back pew for close
to an hour, she started home. It was a little past dusk.

Mr. Sweeney was preparing to close up the shop. She
could see him through the window, counting out the cash
from the register and sorting it into neat piles fastened with
rubber bands. She rapped lightly on the glass. The small
man looked up from the counter, then waved as Mrs. Cribbins started down the dark alley to the back stairs.

About halfway up, she stopped to look for her key.

"Bless me! I've forgotten it," she mumbled, poking
through the loose change at the bottom of her pocketbook.
She held it open, but there was no light at the top of the
stairs.

"I was sure I put it in here," she muttered, turning back to get Sam to let her in. A few steps down she stopped. Something was hissing at the foot of the stairs. She squinted through the darkness, still fumbling in her bag for the key.

"Who is that? Who's there?" A hand darted through the railings and grabbed her by the foot. Mrs. Cribbins slipped her foot from the shoe and scrambled up the stairs. She rummaged frantically through her bag. Then the footsteps sounded behind her. Her fingers touched the toothed edge of a metal key. She let the bag drop and jammed the key in the lock. Something grasped at the hem of her coat. Yanking the door open, she tugged free and then slammed the door behind her. The phone was ringing. She flicked on the light and leaned against the wall. When she caught her breath, she walked unsteadily to the other room to answer it.

"Mrs. Cribbins," Maxine spoke excitedly, "Nora and I are going to stop them!"

"Don't be foolish," the old woman answered, breathing heavily. "You don't realize what you're up against."

"Maybe not, but we have to try! And we can't waste any more time!"

"But it's hopeless. You don't have a chance." Mrs. Cribbins told her what had just happened on the stairs.

"Mrs. Cribbins, I believe they can be stopped."

"And I think you'd be foolish to try, wait . . ."

"Wait for what?" Maxine interrupted. Her voice was

edged with anger. "Wait until they get everyone in Covendale? Mrs. Cribbins, there isn't any time to wait. Nora heard her father say it was becoming an epidemic." Maxine began to explain her theory. The housekeeper listened quietly as Maxine told her of their plan to trap Martin in a lighted room. But they needed Mrs. Cribbins's help. Someone had to distract Mr. Craven. "Mrs. Cribbins, we can't do this without you," Maxine pleaded. "Please say you'll help us."

"What if it doesn't work?"

"That's the chance we have to take. Please, Mrs. Cribbins."

"It's a great risk. You'll have to promise me you'll be careful."

Maxine sighed with relief. "Thank you, Mrs. Cribbins." She spoke quickly before the old woman could change her mind, "We've planned it for Thursday, Halloween. I'll explain later. Mom just came home." Maxine said good-bye and hung up. Halloween was only a week away, barely enough time to work out all the details.

*

The following Sunday afternoon, Nora's parents dropped her off at Maxine's house on their way to the hospital. Nora had seemed so depressed, her parents thought it was best not to leave her alone in the house. When they suggested she spend the night, Nora jumped at the chance to work out the plan with Maxine.

After parking the car, Mrs. Lane went to her son's room alone while her husband stopped by the front desk. The outbreak of the strange affliction had reached epidemic proportions. Over the weekend Dr. Lane had attended nineteen new cases. A specialist in communicable disease had been called in from the National Institutes of Health in Washington, D.C. Dr. Lane was glancing over the specialist's notes when his wife entered Tony's room.

A screen had been set up inside the door to block out the light from the hall. Mrs. Lane hung her coat on the back of the door and leaned quietly against it for a moment, closing her eyes to adjust her vision to the dark room. She calmed herself and gathered her strength before facing her son. The past week had taken its toll.

As she stepped quietly around the screen, the red call button winked from the wall beside the bed. An odd sound, like the hiss of a vaporizer, came from across the room. The air had a sweet musty scent, and a luminous vapor drifted out from the closet. Mrs. Lane crossed the room and slid the door open.

Tony sprang from the floor of the closet and crouched beside the bed. A girl not more than fifteen years old lay crumpled in the corner. She was wearing the uniform of a nurse's aid. Her head lolled to the side. Mrs. Lane stooped quickly and held the girl's wrist. Her pulse was weak and her skin felt like ice. Tony's mother glanced at him in horror. The boy glared at her in a fury, anxious to return to his prey. His mother fled from the room and ran down the corridor to the nurses' station.

"Laura" — she addressed a small broad woman in a white uniform — "there's a girl in Tony's room, an aide. There's something wrong with her."

The nurse abruptly rushed toward Tony's room. Mrs. Lane walked quickly back to the front desk. Her husband was on the phone. She looked pleadingly at him.

"But I'll have to send them out to a commercial lab for those tests, Dr. Norris. We just don't have the equipment here." Dr. Lane nodded at his wife, then spoke back into the phone. "You realize, it will take several days. Fine. I'll talk to you in the morning." He hung up. "What is it?"

"An aide. I found her collapsed on the floor of Tony's closet." His wife's voice was strained and small. Dr. Lane frowned, moving ahead of her toward Tony's room. Two orderlies were carrying the girl on a stretcher out into the hall. The girl suddenly came to. The nurse, Laura, put a restraining hand on her shoulder. The aide pulled away, leaping to the floor with the agility of a cat. The flesh on her face and arms began to erupt in a blistering rash. Shielding her eyes from the light, she darted through a door at the end of the corridor. Mrs. Lane reached for her husband's arm. He turned to face her, brushing the sweat from his brow with one hand.

"Mark, what is it? What happened to her?"

The nurse and the two orderlies rushed to the exit after the girl.

"They'll need help," Dr. Lane said distractedly. "You'd better go on home."

"That girl. I found Tony crouched over her. Please, Mark, tell me what's happening." His wife's voice came in short gasps. She was trembling.

"I don't know." They had reached the door to Tony's room. "Please, Janet. It's better if I go in alone." When she made no move to go, he took her hand. "It's all right. I'll call you. Go on home."

"Tony did it," Mrs. Lane said flatly. "I don't know how, but he did. I know it, Mark."

Dr. Lane nodded, then squeezed her hand.

"Janet, there's something else. I didn't want to upset you, but I think you ought to know. I ran into Officer Pratt this morning. He was on his way in to visit his son. He told me that Cecil hasn't been seen at the dump for over a week, possibly longer. They think he might just be off somewhere on a drunken binge. That may be all there is to it. But I wanted you to know." Dr. Lane waited for his wife to reply.

After a moment, she said nervously, "Then what Nora said about Cecil . . ."

"We just don't know. But I want you to be careful." Dr. Lane held his wife's arm. She shuddered.

"Why don't you go home?" He handed her the car keys. "Try to get some sleep."

"What about you?"

"I'm used to this, remember?"

She nodded and took the keys. "You'll call me about Tony?"

"I promise. As soon as I know anything. Better not talk about this to Nora. Or that business about Cecil, either. I don't want her any more frightened than she already is."

Mrs. Lane walked briskly down the corridor. She was not looking forward to returning to an empty house. For a moment she thought of picking up Nora, but she knew if she did it would worry her. Reluctantly, she drove home alone.

15

A Sudden Storm

By Monday afternoon, it was raining again. Whatever horror was breeding in Covendale, the climate seemed right for it. Attendance in Nora's school was dropping daily. News of the disease had spread through the town, keeping most people indoors.

Nora's night with Maxine had lifted her spirits. Their plan was now airtight, and she was feeling stronger. With the same defiance that Maxine had felt two days before, Nora stopped in front of the Craven house on her way home from school. She glared up at the darkened windows. Three more days, she thought to herself. Only three more days. She turned and crossed the street toward home.

Nora opened the front door and stepped inside. The hall was in semidarkness. "Mom?" she shouted up the stairs. She listened for the peck of her mother's typewriter, but the house was still. She dropped her books and the overnight bag on the table by the door and walked out to the kitchen. The blind to the window above the sink was still drawn. Nora opened the lid to the ceramic cookie jar and thrust her hand to the bottom. There were only crumbs. This surprised her, since it was always at least half full. Her mother usually had the shopping done by Monday morning. Something moved across the floor above her, in her parents' room. Nora set the lid on the jar and walked back out to the hall.

"Mom?" she called again, then started up the dark stairs. The bare branches of a small elm rapped against the window at the end of the hall. The late afternoon was turning to dusk. Nora walked down to her parents' door and opened it. The room was in darkness. The heavy drapes were drawn across the window, which was open slightly. Nora's eyes strained to focus on the bed. She could vaguely make out her mother's form.

"Nora? Is that you?" Her voice sounded strange, weak and wispy.

"Yes, Mom."

"Come here. Sit by me on the bed."

"Why is it so dark in here? Mom, are you all right?"

"I'm just tired. Come here, dear."

Nora moved to the side of the bed and sat down. "How was Tony, Mom?"

"The same." Mrs. Lane slid her arm around her daughter's waist. "Why don't you lie down and take a nap with me?"

"I'm not tired." Nora wriggled free. "Mom, are you sure you're O.K.? You sound awful."

"I think I'm coming down with your cold. How was the night with Max?"

"It was great. I wish we could do that more often."

"Why don't you invite her to stay here?"

"When?"

"Anytime."

"Can she stay Thursday?"

"It's fine with me."

"Great. I'll call her right now and ask her." Nora felt for the phone by the bed, then reached for the lamp. Her mother touched her arm.

"Why don't you call her from downstairs, honey? I want to sleep a little longer." Mrs. Lane rolled to her side and pulled the quilt up to her shoulders.

"Can I get you anything? A glass of water and some aspirin?"

"No dear, I'm all right. Go make your call."

*

Two hours later Dr. Lane phoned. "Where's your mother?"

"She's in bed, Dad. I think she's still sleeping."

"Good. She needs the rest. Don't wake her."

"How's Tony, Dad?"

"He's holding his own." Nora knew when her father used that expression, he usually meant "no better." "Nora, when your mother gets up, ask her to call me at the hospital."

"Aren't you coming home for supper?"

"I don't think so. I'm supervising some tests for the doctor from Washington. Listen, if your mother doesn't get up soon, why don't you go ahead and fix something for yourself?"

"Dad, is something wrong with Mom?"

"No, she's just tired. She hasn't been sleeping well. If you're not up when I get home, I'll see you in the morning."

An hour later, Nora began to feel hungry. She returned to the kitchen and had something to eat. After doing her homework she went to bed, leaving the lights on in the hall and in her room. She slept soundly till the storm broke, an hour before dawn.

The thunder cracked so violently that the glass shook in the windows. The rain pounded on the roof and cascaded noisily over the flooded gutters and into the yard. Nora groggily pushed herself up and walked out to the hall, wrapping her robe around her. The light she'd left for her father was still on. Where was he, she wondered with an anxious twinge. He hadn't spent a whole night at the hospital in years. She walked to the living room and looked out at the street. Although it was close to morning, outside the house was black. The disc of light from the street lamp rippled over the flooded street. Beyond it, a faint glimmer of light shone from a second floor window in the Craven house. It must be Mr. Craven's room, Nora thought. She flicked out the light in the hall and stopped in the kitchen for a glass of water. When she turned off the faucet, she heard footsteps coming lightly down the stairs. Nora walked to the kitchen doorway.

"Mom?"

A hand darted from the dark hall to her shoulder. She dropped the glass and it shattered on the floor. Nora caught her breath as her mother clutched her tightly. Suddenly the hall light flicked on.

"Mom, you frightened me!"

"You frightened me, too, popping out of the kitchen like that." Her mother's breath came in short gasps. They looked at each other, then broke out in nervous laughter.

"How are you feeling?"

"Better." Mrs. Lane yawned. "The storm woke me. When I looked at the clock I realized I'd been sleeping since you came home from school. I was worried about you. I was just on my way to your room."

"Why were you worried? I'm O.K."

Her mother pulled her close again. "I know." She hugged her, then let go and regarded the floor. "Look at this mess." She surveyed the scattered glass. Nora stooped to pick it up.

"Don't, Nora. I'll get it. You're in your bare feet."

Nora dutifully moved back into the kitchen.

"Dad didn't get home yet, did he?"

"No. When I woke up I called the hospital. He just finished work a few hours ago. They said he was sleeping there."

"He hasn't done that in a long time," Nora commented, looking curiously at her mother.

"I know, dear, but this was important. He's running some special tests that have to go out to a lab in Boston today. Nora, could you put the kettle on? I need something hot. My throat feels like sandpaper."

"You don't sound as bad as you did when I got home from school."

"The rest helped. Are you going to have something with me?" Nora's mother emptied the dustpan of broken glass and opened the refrigerator. "Damn. I never did do the shopping."

"There's some ice cream in the freezer. That's what I had for dinner."

Nora's mother groaned and let the door swing shut.

"Now I know why I didn't get up for dinner." She poked through the cupboards and took out a box of crackers.

16

Halloween

THE RAIN CONTINUED for three more days. On Thursday, Nora's father drove to Boston to pick up the results from the lab. Nora's mother went with him, knowing Maxine would be spending the night and Nora wouldn't be alone.

Only about half the class showed up for school that day. Everyone but Nora and Maxine was talking about Audrey's party. Nora worried most of the day about all the small children who would be out on the streets that night. There would probably be widespread attacks, and many more absences tomorrow.

During recess, she and Maxine overheard some of the younger kids griping because their parents weren't going to let them out. If only everyone would just stay in, Nora thought. If she could only warn them.

After school, Maxine and Nora hurried to Nora's house. The time was three-thirty, less than two hours until nightfall. Nora's parents wouldn't be back before six or seven, which fit their plans perfectly.

"Let's go over it one more time." Maxine sat next to Nora in the window seat. "After Mr. Craven answers the door, I ask to use the bathroom. You're positive it's right off the kitchen?"

Nora nodded, staring through the drizzling rain at the old gray house.

"O.K. So once I'm in the bathroom, I help you crawl inside. Then, while Mr. Craven sees me out, you find some place to hide. Then I walk to the end of the street, cut back through the woods, and come in here to call Mrs. Cribbins. Then Mrs. Cribbins will call Marty's father and tell him she needs to see him. And remember, if he doesn't leave right away, get out of there as fast as you can. If he finds out what we're up to, it'll botch the whole thing."

"Don't worry. I'm not going to stay in that house a minute longer than I have to."

"All right. I'll be watching from here. I'll come over as soon as he drives off. That gives us about an hour to find Marty. If Mr. Craven leaves Mrs. Cribbins before we're done, she'll call us over there. I'll pick this up when I come back." Maxine left a flashlight on the window seat and stood up. "Ready?"

As soon as Maxine had slipped into her costume, Nora followed her out the back door and across the yard through the trees. Maxine's costume was nothing more than an old sheet with two holes for eyes. They decided on this because it concealed her completely and allowed her the most movement. They walked along the brook that ran behind Nora's house, staying well behind the trees. Several yards from where the brook turned they came to the intersection of Willoughby and High streets. Here the girls walked out of the woods and parted. Maxine in her sheet, carrying an empty shopping bag, walked slowly down Willoughby back toward the Craven house. Meanwhile, Nora crossed the street and entered the wooded area at the end of the block, quickly making her way toward the Cravens' back yard. Keeping her eyes on the windows at the back of the house, she darted from tree to tree, gradually moving up to the hedges beneath the bathroom window.

As Maxine started up the stairs, she stepped on the edge of the sheet, drawing the eyeholes away from her face and nearly yanking it off. She quickly readjusted it, then rang the bell. When there was no answer, she suddenly wondered what they would do if Mr. Craven wasn't home. The possibility had never occurred to them. She rang the bell a second time, peering through the window at the side of the door. There was no sound from inside. She was about to go back down the steps when Nora appeared at the corner of the house. Flattening herself against the outside wall, she crept to the side of the stairs.

"What's the matter?" she whispered.

"I don't think he's home. I rang twice."

"He must be home. His car's in the driveway. Maybe the bell is broken. Try knocking."

Maxine waited till Nora disappeared around the side of

the house, then knocked loudly. This time, after a short wait, she could hear footsteps coming from inside. The door opened slightly. Hartford Craven looked quizzically through the crack.

"Trick-or-treat!" Maxine said cheerfully, holding out her bag. Mr. Craven continued to stare, looking baffled.

"I know it's awful early, but my parents didn't want me out after dark on Halloween," Maxine said in a rush of words. She stooped beneath the sheet, feeling painfully self-conscious. Mr. Craven's dull eyes looked closer.

"Halloween?" He scratched the side of his jaw. The stubble covering his coarsely lined face made a bristling sound. His hair was matted and he looked as though he hadn't changed in weeks.

"What day is it?" he asked hoarsely.

"Thursday, October thirty-first," Maxine answered rather loudly, growing impatient. For a moment he just stared. Calm down, Maxine told herself, or you're going to blow your cover.

"Halloween?" he repeated, this time as though the word was beginning to make some sense. "Yes, I guess it is. I'm sorry. I haven't anything to give you." He spoke slowly, as if he was only half awake.

"Mr. Craven, can I use your bathroom? I don't think I can wait till I get home."

"The bathroom? Yes, yes, of course." He opened the door wide, standing to one side. "It's through the kitchen at the end of the hall, on the left."

Maxine held the sheet up so she wouldn't trip on it, then stepped into the house. Mr. Craven followed her down the hall.

"Over there." He pointed to an open door, then sat down at the kitchen table. Maxine could see the room was still in utter disorder. She closed the door behind her and turned the lock. Then she pulled off the sheet and hung it over the doorknob, making sure the keyhole was covered. She turned on the faucet, hoping the sound of the running water would cover up any noise she might make. Next, she unlatched the window and pushed it slowly open. Nora's fingers immediately appeared over the edge of the sill.

"Use your feet to push yourself up the side of the house while I pull," Maxine whispered out the window. She took her friend's hands and slowly began to draw her up. When Nora had one knee on the sill, Maxine put her arms around the other girl's waist and carefully pulled her in. Nora closed the window behind her, then stood to the side of the door. Maxine was already back under the sheet.

"Good luck," Maxine whispered, squeezing Nora's hand. She turned off the faucet, flushed the toilet, and left, closing the door behind her. Mr. Craven was sitting in the same place with his head in his hands.

"Thanks, Mr. Craven." Max paused awkwardly, waiting for him to show her out so Nora could find a better place to hide. The man looked up. His eyes were bloodshot and puffy with blue half moons beneath the lids. He looked as though he hadn't slept in days.

"Can you let yourself out?"

Not knowing what to say, Max nodded and departed. She was tempted to run back to the side of the house to check on Nora, but walked up the street and backtracked through the woods as planned.

Hidden by the trees, she tore off the sheet and ran. She called Mrs. Cribbins the moment she got in the door.

"She's in! You better call right away!"

*

Nora was kneeling at the door with her eye to the keyhole. She was trapped. Mr. Craven hadn't budged since Max left. Nora couldn't see his face. His back was to the door. Her knees were beginning to ache against the hard cold tiles of the bathroom floor. What if something went wrong, she thought. Had she forgotten to leave the door to her house unlocked? Maybe Maxine couldn't get back in. The minutes passed like hours. What if Maxine had to run all the way home to call Mrs. Cribbins? She wished she could remember if she had left the door unlocked. The more she thought about it, the more she was sure she hadn't. And what if Mr. Craven needed to use the bathroom? He could walk in at any moment. There would never be enough time to get back out the window without getting caught. Nora's palms began to perspire. She decided to lock the door, just in case. Very slowly, she began to turn the hand lock. It clicked as the bolt slid from the door. Her hand froze. She pressed her eye back to the keyhole. Mr. Craven's head was turned and tilted to one side. He was listening. Slowly, he got to his feet and started toward the bathroom. Nora backed away to the window. She put one palm under the frame, ready to push up. Miraculously, the phone rang.

As the footsteps retreated on the other side of the door, Nora sank to the floor. Every pore was open in a cold sweat. She could hear him talking on the wall phone in the kitchen.

"I can't leave the boy, Ingrid. I've got to be here in case he needs me." There was a silence. "All right, but I can't stay long. He should be waking up soon."

Nora glanced out the window. Storm clouds crept across the horizon. It would be dark in less than an hour. She heard the phone fall into its cradle. Mr. Craven's footsteps grew fainter. Then came the dull sound of a closing door. Quietly, Nora slipped from the bathroom and crept into the hall, glancing up the stairs and praying she wouldn't run into Martin before Maxine got there. Hiding behind a curtain, she watched Mr. Craven get into his car and back it out of the driveway. Just as it turned up the street, Nora spotted Maxine coming out the front door of her own house. She ran across the street and up the walk. Nora unlocked the front door and pulled it open.

"Are you all right?" Max whispered.

"Yes. Come on, we can't waste any time. You go first, you have the flashlight." Maxine led the way upstairs, Nora following close behind. Every few steps the old staircase creaked. By the time they reached the top, Nora's knees felt weak. The hallway on the second floor ran in two directions. There were two doors and a window at the left of the stairs, and four more doors at the right. Only one was open. It was the door to Mr. Craven's room.

"Which way now?" Maxine whispered.

"That's Marty's room down there." Nora led Maxine to a door at one end of the hall, then stooped and peered through the keyhole. She could just make out a pile of bedclothes on the floor and a pennant pinned to the wall. Crimson felt with gold letters. COVENDALE JUNIOR HIGH. Nora quietly backed away.

"I can't see much," she whispered to Maxine, who reached for the doorknob and slowly turned it till the door clicked open. Immediately, she flicked on the flashlight and started inside, waving the light through the room. Nora followed close behind, pressing back on the door till it closed. She blindly swept her hands over the wall in search of the switch. A light flashed on overhead. Three trays of food sat rotting on a corner table. Clothing was pulled from the hangers into a nest on the closet floor. It was like the den of an animal.

"The window," Nora whispered. There was a slight motion behind the drapes.

"Block the door," Maxine whispered back, then quietly crossed the room. When Nora had a small dresser pushed securely against the door, the other girl yanked the curtain aside. A fresh cool breeze poured in through the open window.

"He's not here!"

"He must have crawled out the window."

Maxine walked back to the door and helped Nora pull the dresser away.

"I don't think so. It's a two-story drop. And anyway, it's still not quite dark enough for him to be outside."

Thick black clouds were building across the sky. There was a rumble of distant thunder.

"He must be in one of the other rooms. We'll have to hurry." Maxine led the way back down the hall. They quickly searched Mrs. Cribbins's old room. The door after hers opened to a linen closet, and the one beyond that led to Mr. Craven's room. The lamp by the man's bed was burning and the curtains were drawn wide. Nora followed Maxine out of the room.

"It has to be this." Maxine turned the knob to the door at the end of the hall. On the other side, a steep flight of stairs led to the attic. The girls climbed up to the landing.

The ceiling here sloped with the contours of the roof, jutting out like a cap over the gabled windows at the front of the house. The wind, stronger up here, rattled the glass in the windows. Pigeons cooed and rustled their feathers in the shelter of the eaves. Nora pressed her nose against the dust-streaked glass. Her own house looked like a miniature, discarded from a Monopoly game. The barren branches of the trees standing at the edge of the yard tossed in the wind. Nora turned from the window and followed Maxine through a small door at the side of the landing.

The attic was in total darkness. Maxine held up the flashlight and switched it on. The room was narrow and deep, stretching off to either end of the house. It had no windows, and the uninsulated roof sloped down to form the walls. A clutter of boxes was piled along the eaves, forming a bare strip of floor, like a corridor. There were footprints in the dust. Maxine motioned for Nora to follow, leading with her flashlight. Using her own small light, Nora cautiously peered over the cartons into the triangular hollow formed by the eaves. As they progressed on either side, a stale musty odor crept in around them. There was no ventilation, and the air was thick with dust.

Nora's small keychain light streamed over the contents of the boxes: old clothing, dishes wrapped in newspaper, yellowed bundles of magazines, and an assortment of books and knickknacks. She followed Maxine toward the back of the attic. One large carton was turned on its side. Woman's clothing spilled out to the floor, probably Mrs. Craven's, Nora thought. Her memory of Martin's mother was dim; the woman had always been sick. Reaching behind herself, Nora touched Maxine, who pointed her flashlight into the box. A small brown spider crept out from beneath a collar of lace. Gently, Maxine lifted the skirt of a dusty green gown that bulged from the center of the box. Nora's tiny light settled on a pale bony hand curled around a furry black mound. For a fraction of a second her heart stopped. She grabbed Maxine's arm to swing the big flashlight around. Martin's hand was draped over Nikki's body. Nora turned away, repulsed by the sight of the dead cat held by Martin as though it were still alive. Then an oddly comforting thought crept into her mind. Something of the old Martin *must* still be there for him to cling to Nikki that way.

Martin's fingers began to twitch as if tickled by the light. Maxine tugged Nora by the elbow, leading her back out to the landing.

"So that's what became of Nikki," Maxine whispered.

"Max, what are we going to do?"

"We can't do anything," Maxine said with frustration. "There's no overhead light. We only have the flashlights, which he could easily knock from our hands. We'll have to bring up lamps. If we flood the attic with light, maybe we can push something up against the door to keep him here."

Nora looked toward the small window. The sky was quite dark. Suddenly the shrill ring of a telephone sounded from below.

"It must be Mrs. Cribbins." Maxine scrambled down to the hall, listened, then ran into Mr. Craven's room. She grabbed for the phone by the bed.

"Yes?" she answered breathlessly. Nora stepped up behind her.

"He just left." Mrs. Cribbins's voice trembled at the other end. "Did you find Martin?"

"He's in the attic," Max answered. "But there isn't a light up there."

"Then leave immediately. You can't do anything now."

"But I thought we could carry up lamps."

"There aren't any outlets up there. Just get out as fast as you can and call me when you get home. Hurry." Mrs. Cribbins hung up. Just before Maxine put the phone back, she heard a second click. Someone else had been listening.

17

The Night Walkers

SEVERAL BLOCKS AWAY, Audrey's party was getting off to a slow start. Many of her guests still hadn't shown up.

"Where's Mimi? I thought you two were coming together," Audrey asked a new arrival.

"At the last minute her mother decided not to let her come. You know what a drag Mrs. Gordon is. She didn't want Mimi out with that flu thing going around." The girl followed Audrey down to the basement playroom. Webs of black thread were draped across the stairs. From the ceiling, Audrey had hung gauzy streamers and black paper bats. The only light in the long paneled room came from candles, which flickered from the hollows of four grinning pumpkins. The total effect was like that of a darkened cave.

Audrey's guests were in the middle of playing "Blind Guess." Each guest in turn was blindfolded and seated at a long table where Audrey had arranged thirteen bowls. The bowls were covered with cloth to conceal their contents. At the moment it was Mariette Parker's turn, and she was none too happy. She cautiously poked her finger into a bowl of something slimy.

"Bet it's cat's eyeballs," one of the boys said and snickered. Mariette jerked her hand away.

"I'm not doing it!" She nervously fought with the knot in the blindfold. "Audrey, take this off of me!"

"Everyone else had to take a turn."

"I don't care! I don't like it! And anyway, you didn't!"

"I can't. I know what's in them all," Audrey said smugly as she loosened the blindfold and slipped it over Mariette's head. Mariette peered into the bowl and made a face.

"It's only a chicken liver," Audrey announced impatiently.

"Why don't we play 'Lights Out'?" someone suggested.

"Oh brother! Not that dumb game!" one of the boys groaned.

"Come on, Henry. Be a good sport." Audrey began to blow out the candles.

"Can't we just dance?" Mariette asked meekly. "I'd much rather dance."

"Never mind." Henry stood up and started toward the wall switch by the back door. "We'll play 'Lights Out,' but I'm in charge of the lights."

"I'd really rather dance," Mariette persisted. A few of the girls agreed with her, feeling the game was too childish.

"Hey, Audrey, come here a minute." Henry was looking out the window by the basement door. Audrey looked over his shoulder.

"Were you expecting anyone else?" Several shadowy figures were standing at the edge of the yard. It was too dark to make out any of their faces.

"A few kids haven't come yet. But I don't think they'd walk around back. Henry, keep the light out." Most of the guests grouped around the window behind her.

"Maybe one of them's Johnnie Cobb," someone whispered. "I heard him saying he might crash it."

"Johnnie, huh. Henry, unlock the door." Audrey whispered, "And everybody move back and crouch down. We'll give Johnnie and his friends a little surprise. Noah, bring that case of soda over here. Our friend Johnnie's going to get a wet welcome."

Audrey and her guests pressed back into the darkened room. Noah passed out cans of soda to most of the boys, who shook their weapons vigorously, preparing to spray the intruders. A few of the guests giggled nervously, but were hushed up when one of the figures passed by the window. When the back door opened, Mariette began to climb the stairs. She hated these games, and the darkness and the silence frightened her.

One of the guests began to make an eerie blowing sound, in a spooky imitation of the wind. She could hear the rustle of her classmates as they formed a circle on the floor below. Then suddenly, a ghostly wailing erupted through the darkness.

*

"What was that?" Mrs. Quinn looked up from her reading. Her husband had his feet up in front of the T.V.

"It's just the kids." John Quinn leaned forward to turn up the volume.

"They're getting awfully noisy. Do you think I should go down?"

"Audrey probably has them playing some sort of game. They'll quiet down."

But the wailing rose in pitch, followed by the sound of things breaking.

"That doesn't sound right. I'm going down." Mrs. Quinn rose and walked down the hall to the stairs. Someone was whimpering below. She rushed to the first floor and out to the kitchen. Mariette was standing by the top of the cellar stairs.

"Is something wrong, dear?"

The girl was trembling. "I told them I didn't want to play." She was backing away from the door. Mrs. Quinn walked by her to the head of the stairs. When her hand hit the light, several figures scurried back from the landing.

She called down to the playroom. "Audrey?" After a moment, she started down. The cellar had suddenly grown silent. At the foot of the stairs the woman stopped and frowned.

"Audrey!" she shouted into the long paneled room. Chairs and card tables were overturned. Soft drinks and food were scattered across the floor. The room was dead still except for the streamers and paper bats that fluttered in the wind blowing through the doorway to the yard. Everyone had gone.

*

"Come on." Maxine tugged Nora by the arm. "We have to get out of here."

Nora stood frozen by the window. The sky was pitch black. A light drizzle spattered the windowpane.

"It's too late," Nora mumbled nervously, gesturing toward the yard. Three children were crossing the lawn below.

"They're in costumes. They're just little kids out for Halloween." Maxine grabbed her by the hand and led her from the room. The beam of the larger flashlight glided over the carpet in the darkened hall. At the stairwell, Maxine covered the light with her hand.

"Turn on your little flashlight," she whispered to Nora. "Why?"

"This is much too bright. If Mr. Craven drives up now, he'll see it."

"But my light's too weak, Max. We need yours to protect us."

"My thumb's on the switch, don't worry."

When the small light came on, Maxine switched hers off. For a moment they just stood by the top of the stairs and listened. Then they started swiftly down. As they reached the bottom, a light knock sounded on the door.

"It's just those kids," Maxine whispered, "but we'll have to go out the back." When they turned toward the kitchen, a muffled scream came from the front of the house. Maxine went to the front door and looked out at the stoop. Two of the children they'd seen were pounding on the door. The third, a small boy in a Batman costume, was sprawled across the front walk. A girl in a white uniform crouched over the child's head. As the smaller boy grew still, his assailant turned to face the other two children on the stairs.

Several other figures appeared at the edge of the yard. Most were wearing pajamas and were barefoot. All moved purposefully toward the two children cowering on the steps.

"We have to help them!" Nora cried. Maxine caught her by the wrist. For a split second they stared at one another.

"Max, we have to," Nora said softly, and Maxine dropped her hand. Nora grappled with the lock, then yanked the door wide. One of the children darted into the darkened hall. The other screamed, caught just outside the door by the girl in white. He was dragged by his feet to the bottom step, but held fast to the railing. Nora reached for his hand while Maxine flooded the stairs with light. The light forced the girl back, but she dragged the small boy with her.

"Inside, quick!" Maxine yanked Nora back then slammed and locked the door. Her light danced over the floor behind them, then froze on the foot of the stairs. Martin snarled as he dragged the limp child back against the wall. The boy they let in had fled directly into Martin's arms. Now he dangled, unconscious, as Martin tried to haul him up the stairs and away from the light. Maxine felt over the wall for the light switch. She snapped it up and down several times. It didn't work. Nora rushed up the stairs behind them and grasped the child's legs while Maxine flooded the stairwell with light. Snarling, Martin released his grip and scurried back upstairs. Nora scooped the small boy up in her arms then followed behind Maxine.

"We can still make it out the back." She led them down the hall through the kitchen, then pressed her ear to the door. Slowly, she turned the knob and opened it. The chain lock slid to the end of its tether, holding the door ajar. Maxine fumbled with the chain, trying to jerk it free. A hand slid through the crack. Then another. They caught Maxine by the sleeve. She began to beat them away with the flashlight. A third hand forced its way through the door and caught her by the hair.

"Help me!"

Nora started forward. The child in her arms began to revive. He wrapped his arms tightly around her neck.

"I have to put you down." Nora tried to set the child on the floor. His grip tightened. "Let go!" Nora yanked the small boy's arms away from her. As she ran toward the door, the little boy smiled. His lips glistened moistly.

Nora grabbed a mug from the counter and began to smash it against the edge of the door. One side of the mug shattered, but she continued to beat its jagged edge against the tangle of fingers snaking through the crack. Maxine threw her full weight against the door, and the fingers slid back into the night. Then she pulled a chair from the table and wedged it under the doorknob. The beam from the flashlight dimmed, then flickered. She shook it gently. "I must have damaged the bulb." The moment she began to unscrew the cap, something flew at Nora's back.

"Max!" Nora spun around, trying to shake herself free. It was the small boy. He was trying to pull her down. Nora slammed her back into the table. The child fell, but he was instantly back on his feet. Maxine twisted the cap back on and beamed the light in the boy's face. He hissed at the flickering light.

"We were too late." Nora's voice trembled. Maxine flashed the light at a sound from across the room. In the comfort of shadows, the small boy stretched his arms out to Nora as if in an embrace.

"We were too late!" Nora cried again. With one arm leveled at the approaching child's chest, she swung out her fist, shoving him back against the counter.

As Maxine scanned the windows above the sink, dozens of hands clawed at the glass and the sash, trying to push the windows open. At the touch of the light the hands fell away. Nora searched the dark walls for a switch, but before she could find it, a scraping sound came from the bathroom. With a sinking feeling, she realized she had left the window unlatched. The door to the bathroom swung open, and Tony stepped into the room. He grinned at Nora, walking toward her.

Maxine grabbed her from behind and yanked her back, waving the light in Tony's face. As he turned away she pulled Nora through a door, slammed it, and turned the lock. Her hand was shaking.

"Where are we?"

"I don't know." Maxine's voice quavered. She laughed nervously. "I didn't even know this door was here till I felt the knob sticking into my back." Nora turned around. She felt for the small light dangling from her wrist and flicked it on. They were at the top of a staircase. A dustpan hung from the wall beside several aprons.

"I think it's the basement," Nora whispered. Maxine switched off the bigger light to save the batteries. The shuffling of feet came from the other side of the door. Together, they started down.

"Max, I can't fight Tony," Nora said almost apologetically.

"It's all right." Maxine put a hand on her friend's shoulder and gripped it tightly. "We'll just stay here till they're gone. We'll wait till morning if we have to." The muffled sounds of Tony and the others crawling through the house came through the ceiling.

The cellar in the Craven house was only used for storage. Behind boxes and old broken chairs, the oil burner hummed. Exhausted, Nora sat down on a musty frayed rug rolled up at the foot of the stairs. She pulled her knees up under her chin and began to rock back and forth. The noises above were subsiding. Maxine set her father's heavy flashlight on the floor and collapsed next to her.

"I can't find a light switch anywhere. Hey, are you all right?"

Nora began to sob.

"Hey, we're O.K. They can't get us down here." Maxine

rubbed Nora's back soothingly. Nora sniffled and sat up.

"Max, I want to go home."

"We have to wait. It isn't safe yet."

"But I don't hear them anymore. Maybe they went away." Nora aimed the beam of the keychain light against the opposite wall. "There must be a door down here somewhere." Now, even the smaller light was growing dim.

"But we can't try going out now."

"Max, my batteries are wearing out."

"It's all right. We still have the other one." The two girls sat in silence. Nora's small light grew weaker, then blinked out. The sudden blackness made the room feel smaller, as if the walls were right up against them.

"Max, turn on your flashlight," Nora whispered.

"It's better to save it in case we need it. Don't worry, we're safe here." Max leaned her head back against the stairs. Nora curled on her side and put her head in her friend's lap.

"I'm so tired. Shouldn't Mr. Craven be back by now?"

"Unless he stopped somewhere. I hope he did. You know if he walked in with the house full of those kids, he wouldn't stand a chance." Maxine's low voice lulled Nora toward sleep. Her mind began to drift. Closing her eyes, she listened to the gentle rhythm of her friend's breathing above her. She did not know that she had been dozing until her head dropped, and suddenly she was jolted awake by Maxine's stifled scream. She could hear a scuffle nearby in the dark.

"Max!" Nora reached beside her. Her fingers touched

empty air. The carpet was suddenly jarred as though someone had kicked it. Then she heard something being scraped
across the floor. Crawling on her hands and knees, Nora felt
blindly over the carpet and along the adjacent floor. *Something* was breathing heavily in the darkness. A thin luminous
stream poured across the room. The air filled with the familiar pungence. When she crawled forward, something
dropped in front of her, followed by the sound of tinkling
glass. Her fingers touched cold metal. She picked up Maxine's flashlight and flicked the switch.

A few feet in front of her, in the dimly wavering light,
Maxine lay sprawled across the floor. Her legs were kicking.
A large dark shape crouched over her like a vulture. The
man held her head up by the hair, then buried his face
against hers. Nora jumped unsteadily to her feet, waving
the flickering light over the man's back. The man rolled
aside, then cowered in the corner. It was Cecil McNab.

His eyes were black and enormous, like an insect's, and
his skin was covered with patches like mold. For a moment,
Nora lowered the light as she crawled across to Maxine. The
crouching man twitched and hissed like a snake about to
strike. His shimmering breath sprayed into the air. When
Nora leveled her light on him, he crawled deeper into the
cellar. Then she saw the stairs leading up to the bulkhead.

"Max!" Trying to pull her friend up, Nora tugged her by
the arm, but Maxine fell back limply. Now the man was
backing toward the bulkhead. Ignoring him, Nora lifted
Maxine's head to her lap. When the man was halfway up
the stairs, the sloping doors flew open.

163

"Cecil?" Hartford Craven's deep voice echoed into the room. A flash of lightning illuminated the sky outside. "What are you doing here? And why was my front door latched? I couldn't get in." Holding a kerosene lamp out before him, Mr. Craven descended. Cecil backed away from the stairs, shielding his eyes from the flame. Mr. Craven pulled a cord hanging from the cciling. As the bare bulb flashed on above the pipes, an agonized cry ripped through the room and Cecil reeled backward. Mr. Craven stepped closer, not understanding. Then the cornered man lunged at him. They fell together, grappling at the foot of the stairs.

The broken lamp trickled a stream of ignited kerosene. Cecil bumped against it. The flames licked his shoulder, then suddenly swarmed over his back like an army of golden ants. Releasing Mr. Craven, Cecil struggled to his feet and crawled clumsily over the stairs, then collapsed outside in a sudden burst of flame.

The puddle of fire on the basement floor quickly burned itself out. Beside it Mr. Craven's body lay motionless. As Nora stood, dazed, Maxine stirred at her feet. Shielding her face, Maxine drew herself across the floor to the bulkhead. Already her skin was puckered with the disfiguring rash. In horror, Nora watched her scurry up the stairs and into the night.

"Oh please, not Max," Nora pleaded. Tears filling her eyes, she picked up the flashlight and started after her friend. Mr. Craven stared blindly up at her as she stumbled through the bulkhead.

Cecil's still body smoldered on the grass. Lightning crackled across the sky, for an instant illuminating the woods at the edge of the lawn. A dozen figures straggled off through the trees. Nora could not tell whether or not Maxine was with them. She raised the flashlight, guiding her way to the street. A cab turned at the corner, blinding her with its headlights, and pulled up to the curb. Mrs. Cribbins climbed out, pushing a bill into the driver's hand.

"Keep the change." She slammed the door and the cab pulled away. "Thank God you're safe. What happened? Where's Hartford?"

"He's in the cellar. Max . . . Max is . . ." Nora stammered, beginning to cry. Mrs. Cribbins wrapped her arm gently around Nora's shoulders and walked her across the street.

"Go inside." She spoke softly, taking the flashlight from Nora's limp hand.

"Where are you going?" Nora asked, sobbing, but the housekeeper was already hobbling across the yard back toward the Craven house. Nora started up her own front step. Again the sky exploded with light, and the thunder followed. Nora closed and locked the door behind her.

18

The Covendale Spore

TWENTY MINUTES LATER, Dr. and Mrs. Lane drove into the driveway. Nora was sitting in the window seat wrapped in a blanket. She had turned on every light in the house. The moment her parents walked in the door, the phone rang. Her father went to answer it.

"What's going on? Is there a sale on electricity?" Mrs. Lane started turning off the lights as she walked around the room. Nora's father stood in the doorway.

"That was Mrs. Cribbins. Something's wrong with Craven. I have to run over."

"Did she move back?"

"I don't know. I'll be back as soon as I can." Dr. Lane rushed out the door.

"Your poor dad. Not a moment of rest." Mrs. Lane crossed the room to her daughter. "Where's Max? I thought she'd be here with you."

Nora only stared out the window, fighting back her tears. Her mother checked her watch.

"I want to stop by the hospital and check in on Tony before visiting hours end. Tell Dad I'll be back in about an hour. Hey, are you all right? You look a little funny." She put the back of her hand to Nora's forehead. "You're a little warm. I hope you're not coming down with that cold again. Why don't you hop in bed?"

Nora straggled to her feet, pulled the blanket snugly around her, and started down the hall. When she got to her room she crawled into bed. A strong wind rattled the window in its frame. Rain beaded across the glass.

"Max!" she cried. "Oh, Max . . ."

*

"Janet, wait!" The nurse called Laura jumped up from her seat at the nurse's station and walked briskly down the corridor after Mrs. Lane. "We've been trying to call you all night," she said breathlessly.

"What is it? Is something wrong with Tony?" Before the nurse could answer she was running down the hall. When she entered her son's room, she found the light on. The boy was gone.

"Where is he?" She wheeled around to face the small nurse coming in behind her.

"We don't know. Around five I came in to give him his medication. I found the room just like this." She gestured toward the open window. "It's the only way he could have left. We've been keeping the door locked."

Mrs. Lane's eyes darted frantically over the room. Rain was splattering over the window sill, forming a puddle on the floor. The nurse stepped around her and pulled the window shut.

"Is anyone looking for him?" Mrs. Lane was growing hysterical.

"We called the police," the nurse answered, gently taking her by the arm. Mrs. Lane pulled her arm away and ran back to the nurse's station. She grabbed the phone from the desk and dialed the Cravens' number. Mrs. Cribbins answered.

"Is Mark there?" she asked abruptly.

"He's on the way to the hospital. The ambulance just left. How is Nora?" The housekeeper asked with concern, thinking the woman was calling from across the street.

"She's at home. Oh, Mrs. Cribbins. Could you look in on her? Something's happened to Tony and I have to wait here at the hospital. Please!"

"I will. Don't worry about her. I'll go right over."

"Thank you!" Mrs. Lane hung up and ran to the emergency entrance to wait. Suddenly, she was aware of a siren. Moments later the attendants were lifting Mr. Craven out of the ambulance. They rushed past her through the swinging doors. Mrs. Lane ran toward her husband as he climbed from the back of the ambulance.

"Mark? What happened?"

"Hartford had a stroke. Why are you here?"

"Tony! He's left the hospital!"

"Wait here." Dr. Lane went through the swinging doors and reappeared shortly after with two more attendants. They followed him back to the ambulance and withdrew a second stretcher. A blanket covered the body beneath.

"Did you come in the car?" he asked. His wife nodded.

"Get the test results from the back seat and bring them to me in Pathology."

*

Ten minutes later they were assembled with seven other physicians and the specialist from Washington. For the next two hours, Mrs. Lane listened to the men argue in medical jargon. At last, they seemed in agreement. Mrs. Lane looked at her husband in confusion.

"I don't understand, Mark."

Dr. Lane exchanged glances with the specialist. Both looked very grave.

"Let me try to explain." The specialist walked toward her. "Someone, please, the lights." When the room was darkened, the doctor removed several glass vials from a sealed metal container. The liquid contents of each was flecked with luminous green particles. It reminded Mrs. Lane of the phosphorescent algae sometimes visible in the sea.

"This is a sample of your son's blood." The doctor placed the vial in a metal rack with the others. "Watch closely." He pulled a pen light from his lab coat and flashed a pinpoint of red light at the vial. "This is an infrared beam," he explained, "but it doesn't seem to penetrate or affect the foreign substance that is in your son's blood. But here," he said as he switched the beam from red to white light, "this brighter, visible spectrum of light begins to make a change." Something was happening to the blood. Its phosphorescence faded and the liquid seemed almost to boil. A vapor swirled inside the tube, and in a few moments a layer of fine gray powder, like ash, floated on top of the blood. "It disintegrates in visible light," the doctor continued.

"Why? What's wrong with his blood?" Tony's mother moved closer to the rack of vials.

"First look here." The specialist removed a culture dish from a second metal container. Again he switched on the red light. "These were grown from tissue taken from your son's mouth."

Mrs. Lane reached behind her for her husband's hand. The contents looked like a delicate moss. Each threadlike projection glowed faintly.

"The original sample was microscopic. I can't even estimate how fast the spores grow." Then the white light was turned on the dish. Immediately, the spores began to smolder, disintegrating into the same fine ash they'd seen in the tube of blood.

"Your son, and all the other children suffering as he is, have become the culture base for an unusually delicate species of fungus, or plant, if you like."

"Now that you know what it is, how soon can you treat

them?" Tony's mother searched the doctor's eyes eagerly. Her husband squeezed her hand.

"We're unfamiliar with this particular plant. No one has seen it before. One reason we took so long to identify it was that we were looking at blood and tissue samples taken under visible light. The spore was disintegrating before it could be seen." The doctor paused, looking at Tony's father. Dr. Lane put a hand on his wife's shoulder and nodded for Dr. Norris to continue.

"Mrs. Lane, after it's invaded the tissue cells, which happens very quickly, even the base changes character. An enzyme secreted by the spore seems to bind with the hemoglobin in blood. When the hemoglobin carries oxygen to the tissues, this spore enzyme is then also secreted into other cells in the body. For a mammal to change over entirely, it probably would take only as long as it takes for the heart to pump one complete cycle of infected blood through all the body tissue. Apparently this thing first enters through the lungs, replacing the oxygen and filtering into the blood."

"You said change over completely. I don't understand. What will you do to change him back?" Tony's mother asked tensely.

"Every cell in these children has been altered. Not just the blood. Their hair, their nails, their internal organs. I misled you by saying base. They are not simply carrying the fungus; in a way, they have *become* it. As yet there's just no way of knowing what would happen to a live host if the spore separates from the cells. You see, a cell doesn't live very long outside the human body. These culture bases are dead. Whether or not the condition can be reversed, only time and more experimentation will tell."

"Whether or not . . . ?" Tony's mother started.

"We just don't know enough yet, Mrs. Lane."

Tony's mother turned toward her husband, tears welling up in her eyes. "Mark, why didn't we listen to her? She knew. All along, Nora knew."

19

The Light Within

Two NIGHTS HAD passed since Nora had last seen her father. Most of the children were under close watch at the hospital, but a few had eluded the searchers. Mrs. Lane and the Boykos were still looking for Tony and Maxine. This left only Mrs. Cribbins for Nora to talk to. After Mr. Craven's stroke, Dr. Lane asked the housekeeper to stay and look after her.

For forty-eight hours Dr. Lane worked feverishly, studying the spore. More tests on bits of tissue samples and glass tubes filled with blood. But there was more to a person than cells, Nora thought, restlessly flipping through a magazine and wishing her mother had let her join the search. Why couldn't they understand? The one thing that was in their favor could not be found under a microscope. The thing Mrs. Cribbins called soul.

When her father told her about the experiment with

light, Nora didn't lose hope. Light still might be the answer, she thought, if only the soul could survive. But her father told her such reasoning was simplistic and superstitious. They couldn't take that kind of risk. It was unscientific. And meanwhile nothing had changed.

"Oh, Nora, come look!" Mrs. Cribbins called from the front of the house. Nora picked her robe up from the bed and plunged her fists into the sleeves. She tied it and shuffled halfheartedly out to the hall. Mrs. Cribbins stepped aside to make room for her at the door. She linked her arm through Nora's. Grudgingly, Nora let her keep it there, but when the old woman smiled down at her, she pretended not to notice.

"Isn't it lovely? The first snow." The white dust seemed to fall from infinity. A gust of wind swept across the yard, teasing the carpet of snow into glistening funnels that spun like ghostly tops. All the world seemed asleep beneath its cloak of white. Nora shrugged and turned back into the hall. Mrs. Cribbins looked sadly after her, knowing she was not much of a comfort to the girl. Nora may be safe, with me to look after her, she thought. But what's the point if one is always so miserable? Mrs. Cribbins closed and latched the door.

From the living room window, the new snow stretched like desert sand, unmarred in every direction. It depressed Nora to look at it. It made her feel even more isolated. And somewhere, out in that bitter cold night, Maxine and Tony still roamed. With dread anticipation, Nora knew it would not be long before one or the other would come looking for her. She snapped on the television set and sank back against the couch, hugging her knees to her chest.

"I'm making myself a pot of tea. Can I get you something? Some cocoa?"

Nora shook her head, staring blankly at the screen while she listened to the tap of the housekeeper's shoes as she hobbled down the hall. When the sound came on, Nora closed her eyes and tilted back her head.

It was a news show. The man was talking about a transit strike in Boston. ". . . and all the fares are expected to double again before the year is out. And now, Natalie Grayson with an update on the latest developments in Covendale."

Nora opened her eyes and stared wistfully at the screen. A news camera panned familiar streets. The film had been taken in the midafternoon, but the streets were already barren. Close-ups showed the storefronts with their signs announcing "Closing by Sundown." Although only two days had passed since Halloween, Center Street looked like a ghost town. The commentator's voice described the eerie stillness of this seaside community.

"It began less than a month ago, with an outbreak of what seemed to be a new form of Legionnaires' Disease. For several weeks, the cause of the affliction eluded local doctors . . ."

"We're on the news again, Mrs. Cribbins."

The elderly woman sat down beside her. "When will they leave it alone? Haven't we heard enough?" Nora only shrugged and leaned forward to listen. The announcer was explaining how the Covendale spore was really just a common mold that had mutated, a change caused by Cecil's many pesticides.

"...as yet it is undecided what to do about those afflicted..."

Mrs. Cribbins crossed the room and shut it off. "I really don't think it's good for you to be watching this, Nora. You've got to begin thinking of other things. Life has to go on."

How can it, Nora thought, with half the kids in Covendale sick and her brother and best friend prowling around at night? How could she think of anything else but Max and Tony? But she bit her tongue and said nothing.

"Where are you going?"

"To bed," Nora replied, starting from the room. "Good night, Mrs. Cribbins."

"Good night, dear. Sleep well."

Nora had hardly slept at all these past two nights, anxiously waiting for her mother's return, or some news from her father. She closed her door and wearily crawled into bed. For a long time, she just lay silently on her side, staring out the window. She listened to the gentle wind brushing the snow against the side of the house, and ached for the companionship of her old friend. But it was an ache mixed with fear, for what would she do if Maxine came? Nora gazed for a moment at the lamp by her bed, then abruptly turned it out. Gradually the tide of sleep washed over her.

"Nora." Her name drifted like a chilly wind through the window. Restlessly, Nora turned in her bed, slowly waking.

The snow had stopped. The night was peppered with stars and a thin silver moon. And there was Maxine, her bright black eyes and silky white skin giving her an eerie beauty. Nora slipped from bed and walked to the window.

"I knew you'd come." She pressed her face to the glass.

Maxine smiled. It was a dark and wintry smile. "It's cold, Nora. Let me in." Maxine tapped on the glass, her hollow eyes pleading.

Nora unlocked the window and stepped back. Maxine pushed it open then slipped lithely over the sill. When she smiled again, something glistened at the corners of her mouth. Nora backed up to her desk, trembling. Maxine opened her arms and streamed toward her.

Waiting till her friend's icy arms were clasped tightly around her waist, Nora flicked on the lamp behind her. Immediately she embraced her friend, holding on with all her might. Maxine hissed, twisting her head around in blind terror, trying to break free. Nora continued to cling while Maxine pulled back toward the window. Her face began to erupt and blister.

Nora shut her eyes and shouted, "Mrs. Cribbins!" Within seconds the tap of the housekeeper's shoes sounded in the hall. When the door swung open, Nora looked at the frightened woman pleadingly. "The window! Lock it! And turn on all the lights!"

Mrs. Cribbins moved quickly and quietly, from the window to the lights. Then together they pulled Maxine down to the floor. Her back arched. Her breathing was harsh and choked. She thrashed her head about violently. Neither Nora nor Mrs. Cribbins knew how long they lay there, hanging on to Maxine.

Then Maxine exhaled deeply, emitting a luminous vapor that swelled above her like a cloud. It faded from green to gray, then fell to the rug like dirty snow. Suddenly, she grew still.

Mrs. Cribbins sat back and stared at them, unable to move. Nora still held her friend, smoothing the matted hair away from her face. She pressed her lips to Maxine's ear and whispered her name repeatedly, as if to urge her back. Finally Mrs. Cribbins stood. Tears welled up in the housekeeper's eyes as she stared at Maxine's still form.

Maxine appeared to be only asleep, with an expression of peaceful innocence. The angry red rash began to vanish, her skin becoming smooth and pale. Nora's tears fell to her friend's face and trickled down her cheeks. Bitterly she recalled Maxine's words: "If I were one of them, I'd want someone to take that risk." Nora closed her eyes.

Gradually, she felt herself drifting, together with Maxine in her arms. Something brushed against her face, softly as the wind. Hadn't the window been closed?

"Nora?" Was it Mrs. Cribbins calling? Nora felt as if she was soaring somewhere high above the room. Again the wind brushed her cheek.

"Nora?" A voice in a dream, Nora thought, letting sound and sensation fade. A cool hand touched her face, drawing her back. Slowly Nora opened her eyes. Maxine was looking up at her, with a confused, bewildered expression. Nora clasped her friend's hand.

"I'm so tired," Maxine said weakly. Slumping forward, Nora pressed her face to her friend's shoulder and cried.

"Nora," Mrs. Cribbins called for the third time. The housekeeper was standing by the window, now open. Her attention was drawn to a figure moving through the trees at the edge of the yard. Behind it, flashlights flickered in the woods. The boy stumbled and slipped down the snow embankment into the shallow brook.

"Someone fell in the brook." Mrs. Cribbins turned and hurried from the room. Maxine sat up slowly as Nora moved to the window. Nora watched Mrs. Cribbins crossing the yard, the beam of her flashlight fixed on a boy pulling himself from the water.

"Tony," Nora said under her breath, then ran to help the housekeeper.